Becoming Rose

MARILYN BOONE

Becoming Rose
By Marilyn Boone

©2016 by Marilyn Boone
All rights reserved.

This book or parts thereof may not be reproduced in any form, stored in or introduced into a retrieval system, or transmitted, in any form, or by any means (electronic, mechanical, photocopying, recording, or otherwise) without prior written permission of the copyright owner and/or publisher of this book, except as provided by United States of America copyright law.

This book is a work of fiction. Names, characters, places, and incidents are a product of the author's imagination or are used fictitiously. Any resemblance to actual events, locales, or persons, living or dead, is coincidental.

Cover Design: Brandy Walker
        www.SisterSparrowGraphicDesign.com
Interior Design: Jennifer McMurrain
        www.LilyBearHouse.com

ISBN-13:9781536934939
ISBN-10:1536934933

Also available in eBook publication

PRINTED IN THE UNITED STATES OF AMERICA

This book is dedicated to the rose, the flower that when pressed between two lives ... lives forever ...

Prologue

*Leopold held his breath as he slipped through the
shadows of darkness
His once beloved country was a stranger to him now
He had no other choice but to escape…or die*

Petrograd, Russia, 1917…

Chapter One

Jeannie Fedorchak entered the world history classroom and slid into an empty seat on the front row. Her eyes swept the blackboard then came to an abrupt halt. Written in bold letters across the top were two of her least favorite words: *Semester Project*. Even her stomach growled in disapproval. The words were much too cruel for the first day of school, especially this close to lunchtime.

While she was curious about the new teacher, Jeannie resisted the temptation to turn around and look at him. It wasn't until after the second bell rang that he walked to the front of the class and she saw him for the first time.

He paused a moment before he spoke. "Welcome to world history. My name is Mr. Trotter."

Jeannie blinked her eyes more than once, checking to make sure the image before her wasn't a figment of her imagination. Instead of the usual jeans and cowboy boots she was used to seeing, this teacher was wearing a pair of pleated gray slacks with a light blue shirt and matching striped tie. She didn't know if her best friend, Emma, would think he was "hallelujah" handsome as she was famous for saying, but Jeannie thought he was at least handsome.

"I assume everyone has seen the posting on the board," Mr. Trotter continued.

Jeannie expected to hear the usual groans of protest, but the room remained quiet. She could only assume everyone was as mesmerized by the new teacher as she was.

Mr. Trotter then stepped over to the blackboard and began writing. "This word is genealogy. Is there anyone who can tell me what it's the study of?"

A voice from behind Jeannie blurted out, "If it's the study of Jeannie then it's my lucky day."

Jeannie made the mistake of looking back in time for Brent Phillips to give her a slow, nauseating wink. Having him in her class had just made it her *unlucky* day.

Mr. Trotter ignored the snickering that followed and walked over to the podium. "I see a Jeanette Fedorchak on the class list. Is this Jeannie you speak of the same person?" he asked, directing his question toward Brent.

Jeannie wished she could render herself invisible as the classes' attention shifted her direction, but Mr. Trotter deserved an answer. After it was apparent Brent wasn't going to give him one, she raised her hand. "That's me, Mr. Trotter. Jeannie is the name I go by."

Mr. Trotter smiled. "Then Jeannie Fedorchak you shall be." His eyes lingered on hers before targeting Brent's again. "If the reputation that precedes you is correct, you must be Brent Phillips."

Brent lifted his chin. "Yeah, that's right."

"I'm sorry to have to disappoint you, Mr. Phillips, but genealogy is not the study of Miss Fedorchak. It's the study of our ancestry. For this semester's project, each of you will be writing about your family's history."

"Not a problem, Mr. T," Brent responded, following it with a smirk.

Despite Brent's rudeness, Mr. Trotter's demeanor remained calm and steady. "Mr. Phillips, you might consider controlling your outbursts and refraining from calling me Mr. T, or you will find yourself assigned an additional project. One you may think *will* be a problem."

Jeannie pressed her lips together to contain her amusement while Mr. Trotter finished taking roll. He may be new to town, but he already had Brent Phillips figured out. She decided she may like the class after all.

It wasn't until school was out and she was walking to her car that Jeannie was reminded of Mr. Trotter and the semester project. The old Chevrolet she drove had been a part of her family longer than she had. Perhaps it should be included in her family history, too.

"Jeannie!"

Jeannie stopped at the sound of the voice and turned to see Emma running toward her.

"I can't believe it's our last year of high school and we don't have any classes together," Emma spouted between breaths once she reached her.

"At least we'll see each other during lunch and cross-country practice," Jeannie said then added with a grin. "You know friends that sweat together, stick together."

Emma laughed as they continued walking together through the parking lot. "We'll be doing plenty of that. I'm just glad Coach Manning is waiting until tomorrow to start practice."

"It is awfully hot out to be running today," Jeannie agreed.

Emma's smile broadened. "Oh, I wasn't thinking about the heat or running. The football team is having their first scrimmage this afternoon, and I would have hated to miss it. Do you want to go with me?"

Jeannie should have known her best friend's thoughts would be on boys. "I think I'd rather get a head start on the project for world history. I can at least start writing about who I was named after."

"I guess I have Jane Austen to thank for my name since *Emma* is my mother's favorite novel. In fact," Emma paused to glance at Jeannie out of the corner of her eye, "I've thought about trying my own hand at matchmaking, like the character in the story."

Jeannie glared at her friend. "Emma, have you forgotten how disastrous her meddling turned out? How she almost destroyed the happiness of those truly destined for each other? She also came very close to losing the respect of the one nobleman who loved her despite all her misguided notions."

Emma rolled her eyes. "You're such a hopeless romantic. I was only thinking of helping you come to your senses. Brent Phillips comes from this town's most successful ranching family, has dreamy blue eyes and wears a size 34 Wranglers. What more could you want?" she defended herself.

"Wake up, Emma." Jeannie waved a hand in front of Emma's face. "In case you didn't hear yourself, you've just recited the definition of the perfect boyfriend for *you*, not me."

"Maybe, but Brent's determined to have *you* as his girlfriend."

"That's only because he's used to getting whatever he wants. I would be nothing more than a trophy to him."

"Hey guys, wait up."

Jeannie and Emma twisted around to see Brent's cousin, Sara, hurrying toward them.

"What do you think of the new world history teacher? I hear he's from New York City." The words spilled from Sara's mouth as if a dam had burst.

Emma's eyes grew wide. "New York! I knew there was something different about him other than the way he dressed."

Sara lowered her voice. "Why would he leave an important city like New York to come teach here in the middle of nowhere? You don't think he's hiding something, do you?"

By then the three of them were standing next to Jeannie's car, its white color obscured by layers of red dust. Jeannie wasn't sure yet what to think of Mr. Trotter and saw no reason to add to the rumors that must be spreading like wildfire by now.

She answered with a shrug. "All I know is I like him."

Chapter Two

Jeannie unlocked the front door to her house to find her faithful golden retriever waiting for her. She knelt down so he could lick her face.

"You've got them all beat, Nugget. You're the handsomest thing there is." She gave him a quick pat then picked the mail off the floor and placed it on the entryway table.

A glimpse of her reflection in the mirror hanging above it made her stop and take a longer look. Her features were so similar to her mother's, the dimple in her right cheek when she smiled, her thick brown hair, and even the upward tip of the end of her nose. Other than her hazel-hued eyes and long legs, she wasn't sure what else she shared in common with her father. She had only been five years old when he died, too young to have more than a few lingering memories of him.

Jeannie knew her mother's ancestry would be easy to trace. Most of that side of the family still lived in the next county. But something from deep in her memories had been awakened when Mr. Trotter read her given name aloud. It began as softly as the breath of a faint whisper, but continued to grow until she could almost hear the familiar sound again. It was the voice of her Grandma Sophia, the only other person to ever call her Jeanette.

So many years had gone by since Jeannie had seen her grandmother, but she could still picture the silvery gray hair that was always pinned up into a bun and the warm smile that was framed by storylines of wrinkles. Jeannie missed everything about her, especially the lilting accents of her broken English when she spoke. Sparkling laughter would often follow that could fill an entire room and the hearts of everyone in it.

Chimes rang from the living room clock, drawing Jeannie's thoughts back to the present. Her mother wouldn't be home from her job at the bank for at least another thirty minutes. While the temperature was still sweltering outside, Jeannie felt compelled to go for a short run anyway. The better conditioned she was, the better she would perform at their first cross-country meet.

Jeannie hurried upstairs to change clothes, and then set out on a course that circled through the neighborhood and around the town square. She could usually count on running to help clear her mind, but remembering Grandma Sophia seemed to have unlocked a flood of other memories into her consciousness, ones that weren't as welcome. They were memories from her grandfather's funeral, the year following her father's. It was the last time Jeannie saw her grandmother, and it was all because of Aunt Maria.

Being Grandma Sophia's sister, Maria was really her great aunt, but as far as Jeannie was concerned, Maria had done nothing to deserve having the word *great* in front of her name. Jeannie and her mother had planned for Grandma Sophia to come live with them after the funeral, but Maria wouldn't have it. Her determination to keep Sophia for herself infected every feature on her face, making her the scariest looking woman Jeannie had ever seen.

When it was time to say goodbye, Grandma Sophia peered gently into her eyes. "Someday you will understand my little rose. I leave my heart with you, but the rest of me must go with Maria. She needs me."

As they hugged, Jeannie had felt her grandmother's heart beating in the same rhythm as her own. How could she not have known her only grandchild needed her just as much, if not more?

Jeannie shook the memory away and turned the corner, waving to Mr. Fitzgerald who was outside tending his prized rose garden. She then increased her speed while she passed a pair of basset hounds noisily protecting their territory. It wasn't until she was halfway down the block before the barking subsided and her feet once again settled into a hypnotic pace. That's when she heard music playing.

Despite knowing better than to make an abrupt stop, Jeannie found herself standing still in front of the house the music was coming from. The deep, melodic sound seemed to reach out and hold Jeannie captive as if it was meant just for her. And then it ended. She waited to hear more, but after a few moments of disappointing silence, she picked her feet back up and started moving again.

As she made the final stretch home, Jeannie saw her mother's car in the driveway and hoped her mother was already preparing dinner. Everything about the first day of school had made her ravenous.

"Hi, Mom," Jeannie said, this time entering the house through the kitchen door.

Her mother stood by the stove stirring what looked and smelled to be spaghetti sauce. "I was surprised you ran today. How was it?"

"Not as awful as I thought it would be. Rather interesting in fact." Jeannie wiped her forehead with a towel then continued, "I heard someone playing classical music."

Mrs. Fedorchak gave a light-hearted laugh. "Are you sure it was classical music? I thought the only *c* word in music around here was *country*."

"I thought so, too," Jeannie laughed with her. "It didn't sound like it was being played from a stereo either. It sounded like it was coming from a real instrument."

Her mother's eyebrows rose in piqued interest. "What kind of instrument?"

"A stringed one of some kind, but that doesn't make any sense. Perry doesn't have an orchestra, so who in this town would play one?" Jeannie asked.

"The university isn't too far from here, maybe someone is taking lessons," her mother offered as an explanation. "You know your father loved classical music. I can still see him sitting in his leather chair, listening to it while he read. Of course, that was before you were born. Then you became your father's music," she added with a smile.

Any mention of her father always made Jeannie wistful, more so now because of all the memories that had resurfaced. "I didn't know that."

Her mother let go of the spoon and took hold of Jeannie's arms. "I'm sorry. There are a lot of things about your father I forget I haven't told you."

Jeannie looked into her mother's eyes. "I hope you'll remember even more. The new world history teacher assigned a semester project on genealogy, and I'm going to need to know all I can about my family."

Mrs. Fedorchak let go of Jeannie to add noodles to a pot of boiling water. "Your Uncle John has lots of information about the MacDonald side."

"That will help, but all I know about the Fedorchak side of the family is that they were from Austria. I'd like to learn as much as I can before there's no one left to ask," Jeannie said, finishing with a touch of sadness.

Her mother's expression had turned somber when she looked at Jeannie again. "I received a letter from Maria today."

Jeannie felt her pulse begin to quicken. "What did it say?"

Mrs. Fedorchak pointed to the paper on the counter. "You should read it for yourself."

Jeannie picked it up and began to read, her head soon throbbing from the blow of Aunt Maria's words. She read them again out loud, "Sophia's health is rapidly declining, and I don't know how much longer she'll be with us. She sleeps most of the time so a trip here would be a waste of time and money..."

"A waste of time and money," Jeannie repeated sharply. "Who does she think she is telling us not to come? We're Grandma's family."

Her mother shook her head. "I've never known anyone with a coarser disposition."

"Well, she does remind me of sandpaper," Jeannie said, thinking she could actually feel grit in her teeth as she spoke.

Jeannie's mother looked away, but as soon as she turned back, Jeannie knew a decision had been made. She had seen determination on her mother's face before.

"We're going, aren't we?" Jeannie asked, though she already knew the answer.

Her mother's expression softened. "As long as I know you won't have any problems being excused from school."

Jeannie was just as determined. "Don't worry, Mom, I'll take care of everything tomorrow."

"Jeannie," her mother started, waiting until she had her daughter's full attention. "You realize that even if we do make it in time, your grandmother has been ill for so long that she may have forgotten who we are."

Jeannie's eyes stayed focused on her mother. "We know who she is, and that's all that matters."

Chapter Three

Getting her homework assignments the next day was easy, but it was also their first day of cross-country practice, and she still had Coach Manning to talk to.

Jeannie was in the girls' locker room getting her shoes on when Emma strolled in and found her on the bench. "There you are. Don't tell me you're in that much of a hurry to ruin a perfectly good hair day."

A smile snuck up from Jeannie's face as she finished tying her laces. "I'm still trying to figure out why you joined the cross-country team."

"To spend time with my best friend, of course," Emma said while hurrying to change into her running clothes.

Jeannie threw her a skeptic look. "I'm sure that's not the only reason."

"Well, I suppose there are a few others," Emma confessed, "though not as many as last night."

It took a moment for Jeannie to recall that Emma had gone to the football scrimmage. "It's too bad you can't join the football team, too," Jeannie teased as she stood up. "Just keep thinking of those reasons when you're heading for the finish line feeling like your lungs are going to burst and your legs have turned to jelly."

"At least you've never had to worry about me beating you," Emma said, causing them both to laugh.

Jeannie suddenly turned pensive. "What worries me is telling Coach Manning I'll be missing some practices next week. My grandmother's health has gotten worse so my mom and I are flying out to see her."

"I'm sorry." Emma's tone shifted to reflect her friend's. "Is there something I can do to help?"

Jeannie shook her head. "Not that I can think of, but I'll let you know if there is. For now let's get in a good run."

Emma led the way out of the locker room to where the rest of the team was gathered in the school parking lot. Jeannie looked around for Coach Manning, but he was nowhere to be seen. "Where's Coach?"

"You mean our new one?" asked a teammate.

Jeannie exchanged puzzling glances with Emma. "What new one?"

"The one taking Coach Manning's place. I thought everyone knew," he added when he saw their confusion.

Jeannie didn't have time to process the news before the side door of the school opened and a figure began running toward them with a clipboard in his hand. He definitely wasn't Coach Manning, yet he wasn't unfamiliar.

"Sorry, I'm late. The office just now gave me the team roster," he said upon reaching the group.

Disbelief held Jeannie spellbound for the next few moments. Despite the shorts and polo shirt, he was still the more sophisticated looking Mr. Trotter, her new world history teacher.

"For those of you who don't know, I'm Mr. Trotter, your new cross-country coach," he announced then gave a wry smile, "and, yes, I expect some fun will be made of my last name. It's much better, however, than a surgeon I once knew named Dr. Hatchet."

A ripple of laughter eased through the group.

Jeannie listened as he began to read each name and check it off.

"Jeannie Fedorchak," he called.

"Here," she answered, glad this time her name was listed as the one she went by.

Once Mr. Trotter's eyes found her, he paused and smiled. "We meet again."

Emma jabbed Jeannie with her elbow after he resumed calling out the rest of the names. "How come I'm in his class and he didn't say anything like that to me."

Jeannie's eyes narrowed. "Thanks to Brent, Mr. Trotter learned very quickly who I was. Plus, I had to see him after class today about the assignments I would be missing."

Mr. Trotter's instructions suspended any further conversation between them. "Since this is our first practice together, we'll take the shorter route around the school and through the park. I decided to go easy on you today, but take my advice and get plenty of rest this weekend. On Monday, the real work begins. As soon as you're ready, you may set out at your own pace."

Jeannie joined Emma in a few stretches then looked over to see Mr. Trotter talking to a new member on the team. It was definitely Jason Butler, but she almost hadn't recognized him. He was much taller now, with lightened brown hair and a tan, evidence of a summer spent in the sun. While they had been in school together since kindergarten, Jeannie couldn't really say she knew him. Jason had always been quiet and usually sat at the back of the room.

"Okay, let's go," she prompted Emma.

Emma was a decent runner, but she always started out at a pace too fast to keep up for the entire course. She was already an easy distance ahead, but Jeannie knew she would be catching up with her by the time they both reached the half-way point.

Expecting to be alone until then, Jeannie was surprised to hear the brittle crunch of dry grass drawing closer from behind. She fought the temptation to turn around and relied on her peripheral vision to identify who it was closing in on her left. Words in the form of a friendly greeting caught in her throat when she realized it was Jason. With some effort, Jeannie managed to release a tentative, "Hey."

Jason looked at her, but only nodded in return.

If she hadn't witnessed him talking to Mr. Trotter, she would have decided for certain he must be mute. But despite his lack of speaking, he appeared to be a pretty good runner which made her wonder why he waited until their senior year to join the team.

Jeannie's thoughts were set aside once she was dead even with Emma. "You must be extra slow today if I caught up with you this early."

"It's what I get for not running all summer," Emma responded between labored attempts to keep going. "By the way, did you happen to see Jason...what's his last name?"

"Butler. And yes I did." Jeannie grinned, knowing what was coming next.

"Hallelujah!" they said at the same time, losing what breath they had left from giggling so hard.

After a chance to collect more air, Emma spoke next. "The toad sure has turned into the handsome prince."

"Forget it, Emma. I'm afraid all your conversations would be one-sided. He doesn't seem to talk much, remember?"

"Who cares about conversation?" Emma joked then almost tripped on the sidewalk they were crossing.

"You're doing great, Miss Spencer...Miss Fedorchak."

Emma's and Jeannie's heads jerked around, startled to see Mr. Trotter running beside them. Neither one had heard him coming. Their legs shifted into slow motion, dumbfounded as he continued past them. Coach Manning never ran with the team.

"So, he does know who I am," Emma panted after he was a few yards ahead.

Jeannie gazed thoughtfully at her friend. Anyone who saw Emma would never forget her. She was as pretty as she was boy-crazy with her layers of strawberry blonde hair and blue eyes, set above perfectly sculpted cheekbones.

Once they returned to the parking lot and got some water, Jeannie retrieved her belongings from the locker room and looked for Mr. Trotter, hoping to speak with him before she left. She saw him standing next to Jason again, only this time they were both smiling. Jeannie was struck by how well they already seemed to know each other.

There was nothing to keep Jeannie from walking over to them, but her normal confidence was missing. This was not only a new coach but a new Jason Butler. And with no thanks to Emma, what if she looked at him and a "hallelujah" accidentally slipped right out of her mouth.

Jeannie walked slowly toward her car on the chance Jason would leave. Then as if reading her mind, she watched him turn and go. Mr. Trotter would soon be on his way back into the school.

"Mr. Trotter!" Jeannie waved to get his attention. She tossed her things into the backseat so she could run to meet him, but to her surprise, he had already covered the distance to her car.

"I hope I'm not keeping you from something," she said with a sudden feeling of awkwardness.

"Not at all, what can I do for you?" he asked.

Jeannie cleared her throat. "Since I didn't know you were the new coach when I got my assignments, I just wanted to tell you I'll do my best to keep training while I'm gone. If my grandmother is as sick as my aunt says, I may not get to spend much time with her anyway. That's if she even remembers who I am."

Mr. Trotter's eyes were gentle. "I have a feeling your grandmother will remember you, and spending time with her is more important than running. Besides, I've studied the team records for the past few years. I'm not at all concerned."

Jeannie felt her cheeks warm with his subtle compliment. "I hope I'm lucky enough to get some information for the genealogy project while I'm there. My aunt and my grandmother are the only ones left on my father's side of the family."

"I see," he said, adding a smile. "Maybe the ladybug that just landed on your shoulder is a sign that you will. They're considered to be bearers of good luck, you know."

Jeannie fought the immediate urge to brush it off. She wasn't used to allowing living creatures with legs to crawl on her skin, even a harmless beetle. "Maybe so," she said, returning the smile. "I guess I should be going home now to start packing."

Mr. Trotter stepped back and chuckled. "Is it as treacherous a journey as it looks?"

It took glancing at her car for Jeannie to realize he was referring to its thick coat of dirt. She had given up long ago trying to keep it clean. "No, the dirt is from our property north of town. I like to go out there as often as I can."

Mr. Trotter nodded thoughtfully before looking at her again. "Well, have a safe trip and we'll see you when you get back."

"Thank you, Mr. Trotter." Jeannie got into her car and drove away from the school, but it wasn't long before she was aware of a strange fluttering in her stomach. She figured it was only her nervousness about flying and seeing her grandmother again. Then she remembered the ladybug and checked her shoulder. It was gone, but maybe what she was feeling was the beginnings of good luck. There was something unusual enough in Mr. Trotter's manner that, for some reason, Jeannie believed him.

Chapter Four

Jeannie hadn't flown since her grandfather's funeral almost a dozen years earlier. She felt anxious, and the demonstration on how to put on an oxygen mask and use her seat as a flotation device only elevated her fears. As the airplane rolled down the runway to gather speed, Jeannie closed her eyes and gripped the armrests.

"Now I understand why Grandma didn't like to fly," Jeannie said once the plane seemed to finish its ascent and the pressure in her ears had subsided.

Her mother gave her an understanding smile. "Sophia would often say if we were meant to fly, we would have been born with wings. Yet I know she counted these man-made wonders as a blessing because they made it easier to see you."

Jeannie allowed the corners of her mouth to curl upward then dared to peek out the window. The ground below was a perfect patchwork of green, gold and brown, stitched with country roads and appliquéd with the occasional rooftop of a house or a barn.

"The world seems so much bigger from up here," she mused.

"That's because it is," her mother responded. "I feel lucky I got to travel with your father and explore lots of other places."

Jeannie was quiet for the next few moments before she decided to ask, "Will you tell me again how you two met?"

Jeannie's mother tilted her head and smiled. "Don't you already know that story by heart?"

"I do, but now seems like a perfect time to hear it again," she pleaded with the hopeful expectation it would help the minutes go by faster.

"All right, if you insist," her mother teased as she settled back in her seat. "Once upon a time our bank was acquired by a larger corporation, and your father was transferred to Perry to be the new executive vice president…"

One look at her mother and Jeannie knew she had taken a step back into the past. She suddenly felt selfish for asking. "You don't have to go on, Mom."

Her mother shook her head. "It's okay, I'm fine."

She laid her hand on top of Jeannie's to continue. "Rumors had been spreading for weeks, about the outsider who was coming in to make big changes to our operation. No one was happy about any of it so you can be sure that he didn't get the warmest welcome when he arrived. I hate to admit I was just as guilty as everyone else, not about to go out of my way to meet him."

"So he came into your office to meet you instead," Jeannie assisted.

"Yes, he did," her mother nodded, "right as I was depositing money into the piggy bank that I was using to save for a cashmere sweater I liked. He glanced at my nameplate first, and then he asked..."

"A penny for your thoughts, Miss MacDonald?" Jeannie was quick to interject at her favorite part in the story, causing them both to laugh.

"I told him a penny wasn't enough to buy the thoughts that came with that piggy bank, but if he would call me Laura, I'd give him a special discount. That's when he begged my forgiveness for not introducing himself. I can still hear his deep but kind voice saying, 'My name is Gregory, Gregory Fedorchak.'"

Jeannie was so engrossed in the story, that at least for the moment, she had stopped worrying about how many thousands of feet up in the air they were. "And what did you tell him?"

"When I asked him what kind of thoughts he was interested in hearing, he said that being new to town, he didn't know of a good place to eat." Jeannie's mother looked at her with a broadened grin. "I'm not sure what came over me, but I told him the best restaurant in town was no match for my chicken and dumplings. If he wanted to come over at 6:00 that Friday evening, I would serve him some."

"That was pretty smooth of him, getting himself invited over for dinner," Jeannie said.

Her mother laughed again. "I don't think that was your father's style. I think he was just genuinely hungry."

She then paused. "I suspect he snuck extra change into my piggy bank after that, because by Thanksgiving, I had enough to money to buy the sweater."

"Would you care for a drink?" a voice interrupted.

Jeannie and her mother turned to see the flight attendant had arrived at their row of seats with the beverage cart.

"I'd like some hot tea. What about you, Jeannie?"

"Orange juice, please."

Jeannie waited until the beverages were served and placed on the trays in front of them before prompting the story further, "And then he proposed on Christmas Eve, right?"

Her mother opened a packet of sugar and stirred it into her cup before she answered. "We were taking a walk through the neighborhood to see the decorations and lights when all of a sudden he stopped to face me. He said he didn't want to spend another day not knowing if I would marry him and make him the happiest man alive. I'll never forget the exact place on Dickson Street."

"Dickson Street?" Whenever Jeannie ran her route through the neighborhood, she always returned home down that street. "Will you show me where sometime?"

Her mother nodded while trying to stifle a yawn. "I'm going to try and rest. You should get some, too."

Jeannie watched her mother close her eyes then turned her head to look out the window again. This time it was as if the glass had been covered by a translucent veil of white. As a little girl, she pretended the clouds were mounds of whipped cream, painting the sky with their ever changing shapes. But from this high up the masses of tiny water droplets lost their canvas, and she found herself trying to create a mental picture of all the houses on Dickson Street instead.

Her mind was halfway down the south side of the block when a pair of brown stone pillars entered her memory. They were holding up the front porch of the house she heard the music coming from. Jeannie tried for awhile to recreate the sound of the melody, but it was of no use. She was as worn out as her mother, and the monotonous sea of white was soon successful in making her eyelids drop.

That's when Jeannie heard it again. The music started out low then grew louder with each measure until she recognized the song. She saw herself standing in front of the house listening to it until a voice penetrated her dreamlike state, and something tapped her arm.

"It's almost time for us to land." Jeannie's mother tapped her again.

Jeannie checked the time on her watch. "It's not 8:00 here, is it?"

Her mother shook her head. "No, flying this far west means we get to go back in time, even if it is only a couple of hours."

"My stomach only cares that it hasn't had dinner yet," Jeannie said as she heard it give a low rolling grumble.

"Hopefully, Maria will have some food prepared for us. I told her the approximate time she could expect us, assuming we get a taxi right away."

The mention of her aunt's name reminded Jeannie of the sobering reason for this trip. Her grandmother was close to dying if she hadn't died already. Jeannie didn't know why she felt like that would give Maria a sense of satisfaction, like she could at last claim her victory. The final tally of years they each got to have Sophia live with them: Aunt Maria, 12, Jeannie and her mother, 0.

Becoming Rose

A shiver coursed through her body as the plane's engines throttled down to prepare for landing. Jeannie fought the resulting lightheadedness the only way she knew how, by holding on to the memory of her Grandma Sophia's beloved face.

Chapter Five

The taxi pulled up in front of a gray clapboard house that was more inviting than Jeannie expected from such an inhospitable person as Aunt Maria. On one side of the house was a trellis of pink climbing roses, dividing a set of windows, and on the other was a small porch with a swing on the end facing the street.

They hadn't taken more than a few steps toward the front door when her mother paused. "Are you sure you're ready for this?"

Jeannie nodded. "I just want to see Grandma."

The first knock wasn't answered, nor the second. Jeannie's mother then pressed the button for the doorbell.

"Mom, what if..." The rest of her words were swallowed by the stooped figure of Maria standing beside the opened door. Only a few inches separated them. Though Jeannie had struggled with memories of what her aunt looked like, the coolness of her glare was immediately familiar. The sight caused all the unresolved feelings from her childhood to come rushing back.

"I thought you might have changed your mind about coming," she said, eyeing each of them.

"The trip from the airport took longer than I anticipated because of the traffic," Jeannie's mother spoke, ending with a polite smile.

The muscles in Maria's face were all that responded, twitching randomly into a variety of disapproving expressions. She finally stepped back far enough to let them in. "Wipe your feet."

Jeannie followed her mother inside. Drapes were drawn in front of the large picture window, allowing only a small amount of light to filter through. In the dimness, Jeannie saw what looked to be an old velvet sofa along with a small number of other worn furnishings that made up the rest of the room's interior. The air smelled just as old, like it had been a prisoner of the house for years.

"I suppose you're hungry." Maria's words were tainted with inconvenience.

"We wouldn't want to impose, but it has been a long time since we've eaten. We'd be grateful for anything you have to offer," Jeannie's mother answered.

"After I show you where you'll be sleeping," Maria said, starting to leave the room.

"Can't I see Grandma first?" Years of having to wait fueled Jeannie's impatient outburst.

Mrs. Fedorchak shot her daughter a look of caution.

Maria's answer was unsympathetic. "That won't be possible tonight."

Jeannie responded to her mother's warning and calmed her voice the best she could, "But that's why we came here."

"We retire early. It's best that she get her rest until tomorrow." The rigid line formed by Maria's mouth remained unchanged as she turned to lead them down a short hallway.

Jeannie slowed down as they passed by a door that was closed. She wished her eyes had the power to see through to the other side so she would know if that's where her grandmother was.

"This is where you'll be staying. I only have one extra bed so you will have to share it." Her aunt's abrupt voice yanked Jeannie's attention toward the room where Maria and her mother were now waiting.

"I'll set some food out in the kitchen while you unpack. You can put what's left back into the refrigerator after you've finished."

"Are you not joining us?" Jeannie's mother sounded surprised they would be dining alone.

"I've already eaten," Maria answered then turned and left.

"I guess I didn't really expect her to have changed," Jeannie's mother said shortly after she was gone.

"Mom, this is crazy. The sun hasn't even gone down, and Maria says we can't see Grandma until tomorrow. We shouldn't need her permission." Anger colored every syllable of Jeannie's words.

Her mother opened one of the suitcases and lifted out a few shirts to hang up in the closet. "Jeannie, there isn't much we can do without causing trouble, and maybe her reasons are valid. I promise we'll see Sophia first thing in the morning. Until then, our only hope of feeling better is to eat something."

The kitchen they entered was right off the small dining area adjacent to the living room. A platter of chicken, a bowl of salad and slices of bread and butter were waiting for them on the table that had been set with plates and silverware. For a while, the only sound that could be heard was the tapping of forks as they ate.

Jeannie leaned back in her chair once she had finished and glanced around the room more thoroughly. "Where do you think Maria went off to?"

Her mother's eyes followed the path of her daughter's inquiry. "There must be another bedroom somewhere, maybe through that door next to the refrigerator. But speaking of beds, sleep does sound heavenly after traveling all day."

The trip had taken a toll on Jeannie, too, but she wasn't ready for sleep. After they cleaned up the dishes and returned to their room, she unpacked a notebook and pencil and propped herself up in the bed next to her mother. It took her a moment to get started, but she soon had an entire page filled with questions about her grandparents she hoped to have answered. Her mother was in a peaceful slumber by then, and Jeannie smiled at how young and pretty she still looked. Only a few wrinkles swept out from the corners of her eyes and mouth on a face surrounded by layers of dark brown curls. There was no question how her father became so quickly smitten.

She turned out the lamp and burrowed deep beneath the covers to find the warmth she was accustomed to. Despite how tired she was, however, Jeannie couldn't keep her eyes closed. Morning was still hours away, and she was worried. What if something happened between now and then before Jeannie could see her grandmother?

A sense of urgency compelled Jeannie to carefully slip out of bed. The joints in her ankles popped as she took her first steps, freezing her in motion for an instant before she dared to continue. Once she was in the hallway, she looked at the door that had remained closed since they arrived. Her heart began to flutter as though it had grown wings and was trying to escape, beating faster with each step until her hand clutched the doorknob. Jeannie tried to turn it, but perspiration caused the metal to slip in her palm. She spread her fingers wide and tried again. This time, with the sound of a click, the door opened.

Jeannie pushed on the knob with cautious determination, every sense alerted to what she might find inside. A nightlight on the far wall provided a faint glow, allowing her to make-out the arrangement of unfamiliar objects in the room. Her eyes darted from one to the other until they landed firmly on the bed. Jeannie felt her heart lurch inside her chest. The figure she was looking at had to be her grandmother.

Creeping closer to her bedside, Jeannie saw only a mere resemblance of the picture she held fondly in her memory. She could almost see through her grandmother's thin skin, loose and shriveled over her bony frame. Her long hair, once always braided and pinned neatly into a bun, was nothing more than strands of gray beside her face. Jeannie covered her eyes, shielding them from the harsh reality.

"Grandma, you can't die," she whispered softly to herself as a tear forged a path down her cheek. Maybe her mother's concerns were right. Maybe she wasn't ready for this.

"Rose?" rasped a barely audible voice.

Jeannie's hands flew off her face to see her grandmother's eyes open and looking straight at her. "Rose," she said again, rocking her head forward as if she wanted to sit up.

Jeannie sucked in a deep breath and started backing out of the room, slowly at first, and then she ran, closing the door behind her. She didn't start breathing again until she was back in the bed beside her mother. The tears were flowing in a steady stream by then as the words fell silent from her mouth, "I'm sorry, Grandma...I'm so sorry."

Chapter Six

Jeannie's eyes opened to a bridge of light over the bed, knowing right away it was morning. She hadn't remembered falling asleep and hoped the thoughts that lingered in her mind were only the remnants of a bad dream. The dampness she felt on her pillow told her otherwise. The tears she had shed were real. Jeannie hurried to sit up, hoping to keep the disturbing image of her grandmother from returning to her thoughts.

"Jeannie, are you all right?"

Jeannie felt her breath suspend when she turned and saw her mother by the window. The way the sun was basking her in its warm glow made the moment seem surreal. It was how Jeannie imagined an angel might look like was she ever to see one.

"Jeannie?" This time her mother walked over and sat beside her on the bed. She placed a hand on Jeannie's forehead. "You're not feeling sick are you?"

"No, I'm fine." Jeannie recovered her voice, relieved to see her mother in a more natural light. "I guess I'm just surprised at how bright the room is."

"Well, I'm not sure Maria would approve, but I closed our door and opened the blinds while I was waiting for you to wake up. Look at what I found on the shelf." Her mother's eyes danced with the delight of someone who had just uncovered a buried treasure.

Jeannie took the old manila envelope her mother handed her and pulled out what was inside. She stared at the black and white photograph in front of her. "This must be Grandma and Grandpa's wedding picture."

She continued to study the couple in the middle who were the bride and groom. Her grandmother was wearing an ankle length white dress and was holding a large bouquet of cascading flowers. Standing tall and proud beside her was Jeannie's grandfather in a dark three-pieced suit. "They look so young and happy."

"They were." Jeannie's mother spoke softer, "Your father was such a spitting image of his own, except for the smile, which came from his mother. I see both of them in you as well."

Jeannie tried to inscribe every detail of their faces in her memory before looking up. "I wonder if Grandma would like to see this."

Her mother smoothed some hair on top of Jeannie's head. "We'll never know if you don't get out of bed and get dressed."

Jeannie hesitated at first, feeling apprehensive about what the day might bring. But after another look at the picture, she hurried to change into some clothes and brush her hair. Her mother opened the bedroom door and stepped out first. As they walked past her grandmother's room, Jeannie swallowed hard. She would have to pretend she hadn't already seen her.

They checked the living room and kitchen for Maria, but she wasn't in either place. Then her mother motioned to her from the front door that stood ajar. As soon as they were on the front porch, they saw Maria tending to the pink rosebush.

Jeannie's mother spoke first. "Good Morning, Maria."

"You missed breakfast." Maria's response snipped as sharply as the metal shears she was using to prune the spent blossoms.

"Then I guess there's nothing to keep us from seeing Sophia right away. Shall we go ahead by ourselves?" Jeannie's mother tone was restrained but firm.

Maria's hard gaze shifted between them. "I'll be right there."

No longer as intimidated by Maria, Jeannie returned the gaze. "May I have one of those roses to take to Grandma?"

Her aunt's mouth started to open then snapped shut as if she knew she didn't have a good enough reason to refuse. She cut a stem bearing both an opened flower and a closed bud and thrust her hand toward Jeannie.

"Thank you." Jeannie took the stem from her, forgetting that the manila envelope was still in her other hand.

"What is that?" Maria's frown bore suspicion.

"It's something I want to show Grandma." Jeannie did her best to act casual, moving the envelope out of sight behind her. She wasn't about to let Maria have the satisfaction of knowing what was in it.

Jeannie and her mother waited while Aunt Maria set aside her tools, and then followed her back into the house.

She continued down the hallway, stopping at the door Jeannie had opened the night before. "I hope this is worth your visit."

Mrs. Fedorchak gave Jeannie an encouraging nod. Jeannie responded with a deep breath and entered the room first. It didn't look quite as ominous with daylight filtering through the window as she walked toward the bed. The declined state of her grandmother was still difficult to accept, though this time the impact was a little softer. Her eyes were closed, yet Jeannie believed she detected a faint smile.

"Grandma," Jeannie said. "Grandma," she repeated a little louder.

She watched her grandmother's eyelids lift slowly at first then spring open once she saw her. "Rose...you came back." Her arm trembled uncontrollably as she tried to reach out to Jeannie.

Jeannie stepped in closer, comforted by the familiar accent and by the secret knowledge her grandmother remembered seeing her last night, even if she was calling her by the wrong name. "Yes, Grandma, I'm here."

"I tried to warn you this would happen, that she wouldn't remember who you are anymore," Aunt Maria chided from the doorway.

Her mother gave Maria a disapproving glance then joined Jeannie beside the bed. "Hello, Sophia, it's Laura."

Grandma Sophia's eyes became fixed on her mother, making Jeannie wish she knew what her grandmother was thinking. Did she really not remember anything about her family... her own son?

Jeannie had almost forgotten about the stem of roses in her hand until one of the thorns poked her finger. "Here Grandma, I brought you something from the rosebush outside."

Her grandmother's face lit up when the pink roses were held in front of her. "They're beautiful."

"Maria, do you have something to put the roses in for Sophia?" her mother asked.

Maria didn't respond until Grandma Sophia looked at her as if she was the one asking the question. By the time Maria returned with a small vase, Jeannie had taken the picture out of the manila envelope and was showing it to her grandmother. It wasn't easy to tell if she even recognized herself or her husband.

"He's...handsome," her grandmother finally said.

"Yes, he is, Grandma," Jeannie agreed.

Without any warning, Maria dropped the vase on the table and grabbed the corner of the picture. "Where did you find this?"

Her grandmother's grip tightened with a resolve much stronger than physical strength as Maria tried to pull the photograph away from her. It became apparent neither was willing to give up. One glance at her mother and Jeannie knew she had reached her limit of tolerance. She watched as her mother threw her hands on top of her aunt's.

"Maria, if you don't stop, you'll destroy it. There can be no harm in Sophia seeing a picture from her wedding."

"I asked you where you found it."

"It was in the bedroom on the shelf. Now, please let go," her mother commanded.

Maria's entire body shook as she loosened her fingers from the picture. "I should have gotten rid of it like I did everything else." Then adding with a cutting glare, "Why did you have to come here and ruin what we had?"

"I don't know what you're talking about, Maria, but I think it's time for us to leave the room and let Sophia rest." Mrs. Fedorchak used her words to drive Maria toward the door.

"Why isn't she coming?" Maria asked when she turned and noticed Jeannie wasn't with them.

"I believe she deserves time with her grandmother by herself." Her mother punctuated her answer with the sound of a closed door.

Jeannie closed her eyes briefly to calm herself. When she reopened them, her grandmother was still staring at the picture. "It's all right now, Grandma. You can look at the picture for as long as you like."

She stayed by the bed wondering why Maria reacted with so much anger when seeing the photograph. And what did she mean when she said she got rid of everything?

When she couldn't come up with an answer, Jeannie's attention drifted to the table on the other side of the bed where the vase of roses was left. She noticed there was a silver hairbrush beside the vase and walked around to pick it up. An *S* engraved on its back left no doubt that it belonged to her grandmother. Jeannie could tell it was old by the places that were too tarnished to be polished, and by the yellowed bristles that were either broken or missing. It was still beautiful, however, in its worn charm.

"Would you like me to brush your hair, Grandma?"

Her grandmother's eyes stayed focused on the picture while she gave a slight nod of her head. Jeannie lifted strands of hair from the pillow and began making careful strokes through it. The repetitive motion was almost hypnotic, helping her to forget the reality of her grandmother's condition and the reason why she and her mother were there.

Jeannie finished one side and started to move to the other when she noticed tears pooled in the corners of her grandmother's eyes. Panic hastened her pulse. "Grandma, am I hurting you?"

Her grandmother blinked, forcing one to roll down her cheek. She shook her head and looked at Jeannie, "I'm just so happy." Then she did her best to point to Jeannie's grandfather in the picture. "He always brushed..."

"Grandfather used to brush your hair?" Jeannie asked, though she felt certain of the answer.

"Yes," she said with her next breath.

When Jeannie finished brushing the other side, she saw that her grandmother had fallen back asleep. The picture she had gripped so tightly was lying on her chest over her heart. Jeannie couldn't imagine a more appropriate place. She sat down in a chair next to the bed and tried to immerse herself in the peaceful aura now surrounding her grandmother, a peace that appeared to be bound to the man she loved.

Jeannie didn't realize she had dozed off until her mother brought in a tray of food. After missing breakfast, she was surprised her hunger hadn't kept her awake. For the rest of the afternoon, Jeannie watched her grandmother come in and out of slumber. Whenever she opened her eyes she would smile at Jeannie then look at the picture before closing them again.

When the door opened the next time it was Maria. "Sophia must eat before I get her ready for the night. Your mother is waiting for you for dinner."

Avoiding eye contact with Maria, Jeannie leaned in close to her grandmother. "I'll see you in the morning, Grandma."

Jeannie considered going for a run after she ate, but chose to spend the evening in bed, reading a book she had brought for her English class. As soon as her eyelids grew too heavy to keep open, she closed the book, expecting sleep to come easier than the night before. Instead, the stillness began to haunt her, and she soon sensed a strong pull coming from outside the bedroom door.

Alarmed at first, Jeannie drew courage from its growing lure and slipped out of bed again, being just as careful not to wake her mother. She knew it was late, but the overwhelming urge to see her grandmother led Jeannie back into her room. She couldn't wait until morning.

Grandma Sophia was lying in the same manner in which she had left her, with the wedding picture resting across her chest. This time Jeannie was able to look past the shell of her deteriorating body and see the life that was still present. It didn't matter that her grandmother hadn't seemed to remember her. At least she had remembered her husband.

Jeannie sat in the chair beside the bed and rested her head on the blanket, thankful to be close to her. Whether one minute passed or several, she had no idea. Jeannie only knew that she must have been almost asleep when her grandmother's fingers brushed against her cheek.

"My rose, my little rose," she said weakly.

Jeannie lifted her head and found herself looking directly into her grandmother's eyes. She started to apologize for disturbing her, but before the words came out, Jeannie heard an echo of what her grandmother had just called her. How could she have forgotten?

"You do know who I am, don't you?" she gasped. "You used to call me your little rose."

Her grandmother's eyelids nodded for her.

Jeannie's throat tightened with emotion. "Grandma, I've missed you so much."

She cradled her grandmother's hand in both of hers before slowly releasing the frustrations of the past. "There's so much I've wanted to know about you and my father..." her thoughts trailed off into silence.

A shallow but labored breath cautioned Jeannie. "You don't have to talk, Grandma. It's all right. Those things aren't important now."

The grip Jeannie witnessed earlier that day took hold of her arm. "There are letters..."

Jeannie fought a rising level of fear from the pressing fingers. "Grandma, please rest. You can tell me tomorrow."

Her plea had an immediate effect as her grandmother's arms relaxed back onto the sheets, and she turned her head toward the vase of roses on the table. "One rose has already had its tomorrows," she said before gathering more air to continue, "but you...you my little rose are like the bud... you will have many more."

Jeannie tried to stop the chill that her grandmother's prophetic words sent through her as she stood to leave. "Go back to sleep, Grandma. I love you."

She hadn't taken more than a step toward the door when she heard, barely above a whisper, "I love you, Jeanette."

Chapter Seven

The bedroom was dark and quiet when Jeannie opened her eyes the next morning. She felt an immediate awareness that her mother was no longer beside her and rolled over to check. It wasn't a surprise to see that side of the bed empty since her mother often had trouble sleeping. Jeannie figured it was still early, but when she looked at her watch, she saw it was already eleven o'clock.

Jeannie launched herself out of bed and pulled up the blinds, noticing everything was as quiet outside the house as it was inside. Yesterday's sky had been bright and cloudless, but this morning's palette consisted of shades of gray, warning of impending rain. If there was supposed to be a calm before the storm, it was having the opposite effect on Jeannie as a nervous undercurrent began pumping through her veins.

Instead of getting dressed, Jeannie grabbed a robe and left the room to find her mother. She couldn't help pausing by her grandmother's door but talked herself out of going in, deciding to wait until she had eaten a piece of toast and taken a shower.

Jeannie found her mother sitting in the swing on the front porch. "You never let me sleep this long."

The corners of her mother's mouth lifted slightly, but the rest of her expression was somber in contrast. Jeannie's already unsettled frame of mind was quick to react. "What's wrong? What has Maria done now?"

Jeannie's mother shook her head then reached out and took hold of her hand. "Jeannie…"

If her mother said anything else, Jeannie didn't hear it. The long black hearse that pulled up in front of the house said everything for her.

"NO!" Jeannie ran back into the house and burst into her grandmother's room. Maria was pacing back and forth in front of the windows and ignored her entrance. Jeannie stared at the foot of the bed until she worked up the courage to look at her grandmother. The sheet had been drawn up under her chin with only her head showing. Though her skin was slightly more ashen, she didn't look as different as Jeannie had feared.

She felt her mother's arms around her as two men came in with a stretcher to remove her grandmother's body from the room. Nothing was said while they followed them outside and stood on the porch, watching as her grandmother was placed inside the hearse and driven away. The clouds must have known it was time to mourn as if in perfect timing, rain began to pour.

"I can't believe she's gone," Jeannie said not wanting to turn her eyes away from the street.

"She would still be alive if you hadn't come." Maria opened the screen door and came toward Jeannie with a pointed finger.

Jeannie's mother rushed to place herself between them. "Maria, how could you say such an awful thing? We had nothing to do with Sophia's death, especially Jeannie."

"Sophia was never as happy as when she talked about Jeanette. I knew she wouldn't die until she had seen her again and once she did..." Maria's shoulders started heaving with emotion as she turned to go back inside.

Tears broke through Jeannie's numbed state and began streaming down her cheeks. "Mom, is she right? Could it really be my fault?"

Mrs. Fedorchak took her daughter's face in her hands. "Listen to me. After your father, you were your grandmother's greatest joy. Think what a gift you gave her by being here. Maria is wrong and too selfish to think about anyone's grief but her own."

Jeannie couldn't contain the sobs any longer and stayed in her mother's grasp till they subsided.

"Let's go in and rest awhile." Jeannie's mother guided her inside and into the bedroom.

She tried to close her eyes but it was of no use. The vision of her grandmother kept renewing the flow of tears that stayed close at hand. But there were also tears of anger mixed in with those of grief. Maria had no right to accuse her so wrongly.

After a long while accumulating piles of spent tissues Jeannie decided to get a glass of water from the kitchen. She hadn't felt like eating, but she was thirsty, and water was the only thing she felt she could manage to swallow. Her steps stopped short when she saw Maria sitting at the table, working on something she held in her lap. Jeannie couldn't tell what it was, only that it must be important the way her eyes and fingers were paying such careful attention to detail. Surely, Maria wouldn't dare speak to her after what she had said earlier.

Jeannie walked to the sink to fill her glass and heard Maria moan. She turned around but was reluctant to respond.

Maria's hands had stopped and her head was bowed. "I can't do anymore."

Jeannie was surprised by the defeated tone of her voice. Whatever it was this brazen woman was making, she was giving up. Jeannie gazed at Maria a moment longer. It was obvious by her red, swollen eyes that she had been grieving just as much.

Jeannie had lost both her grandparents and her father, but losing a sister couldn't be any easier. She felt her anger lesson ever so slightly. "Is something wrong?"

Maria lifted up the object to where Jeannie could see it was a small rectangular pillow. "This must be finished, but my eyes are weak and my fingers are no longer nimble."

Jeannie would have appreciated an apology, but set her glass down and sat in a chair beside her. "Is there something I can do to help?"

"You can sew this," she answered, pushing the object in front of Jeannie.

It wasn't until then that Jeannie saw the needle and thread. "Oh no, I can't sew. Maybe my mother..."

"You...you must try." Maria's next breath appeared to be hinged on Jeannie's willingness.

Jeannie was confused by the sense of urgency. "Why are you making this?"

Maria's answer dripped with sorrow. "It's for Sophia. It's the pillow I promised I would make for her casket."

The mention of her grandmother's name made the ache in Jeannie's chest return. She looked at the object requiring them to work together to fulfill a simple request for someone they both loved. "I suppose I can try to sew if you'll show me how."

"Just keep pulling the needle through both layers of fabric until the opening is closed. You can see what I've tried to do." Maria showed her the stitches she'd already sewn.

Jeannie took hold of the pillow then picked up the needle to attempt to make her first stitch. "I've never seen stuffing like this before."

Maria shook her head. "That's because it's your grandmother's hair."

The pillow flew from Jeannie's hands onto the floor. She stared at it for a few seconds before hurrying to pick it up and brush off any dirt. "I...I had no idea," she stammered.

The look on Maria's face grew distant. "Every morning and every night Sophia would brush her hair. Each time she finished, she pulled out the strands from the bristles and saved them. Later, when the brushing became too difficult, I did it for her."

Jeannie let the information filter into her thoughts. "I don't understand. Why use her hair?"

"Sophia called it her crown of glory. She said her hair was a gift she must take to her grave." Maria let silence settle in before she stood up and left the kitchen, going through the door Jeannie had already suspected led to her bedroom.

Jeannie's thoughts went back to the day before when she had brushed her grandmother's hair. Any strands that were left in her brush would now be in this pillow. Her fingers reached inside the opening to touch it one last time. Its texture was just like Grandma Sophia, warm and soft, with the hint of a curl that reminded Jeannie of the twinkle in her eye.

She picked up the needle and thread again and did her best to finish sewing the case that held her grandmother's crown. It may not be one of gold and jewels, but to Jeannie it was one of even greater value.

Chapter Eight

It felt strange for Jeannie and her mother to be leaving so soon after her grandmother's death, but there was no reason to stay any longer. All of the details for Sophia's funeral had been taken care of. Her body would be flown across the country to the east coast and buried in the cemetery next to her husband. A small service would be held at the same Russian Orthodox Church they used to attend, where her grandfather's service was held all those years ago.

With the suitcases ready at the front door, Jeannie pushed aside the drapes once again to see if the taxi had arrived. This time the draw cord swung against her cheek, provoking her to grab it and yank with both hands. *Enough of this depressing room...this whole depressing house* she wanted to scream. Her arms shook as the drapes stalled before opening with a jerk. All at once, the color that had been dimmed by darkness rushed to meet the light now streaming in.

Despite the spray of dust that filled the air, Jeannie found herself looking at everything as if it were for the first time. The drab looking sofa was actually a warm, rich shade of burgundy, and was flanked on either side by wooden tables and brass lamps that seemed to shine with new life. It looked more like a *living* room now. While she wouldn't have broken the cord intentionally, she wondered how awful it would be if she had.

"So this is what this room looks like in daylight," Jeannie's mother said walking into the room. She followed the same path of discovery as Jeannie had, touching the sofa first, then the needlepoint cushion of the rocking chair before joining her. "I'm surprised Maria opened the drapes."

Jeannie started to confess what she'd done when the cover of an old magazine suddenly distracted her. She picked it up off the coffee table to get a closer look.

"Mom, look at this." She pointed to the address label.

"Maria Winston," her mother read aloud then shrugged her shoulders. "That's odd. Why would she use a different last name? Unless…"

Jeannie finished her mother's sentence, "…she was married?"

Their eyes caught each other's as they said in unison, "Impossible."

"What's going on in here?" Maria burst into the room and rushed toward the drapes as if her very life was being threatened. "Why are these open?"

"Don't you think you would enjoy the room more if it were a little brighter?" Jeannie's mother attempted some optimistic persuasion.

"No…no," she answered, fumbling to pull the right cord.

Jeannie placed the magazine back onto the table. Though bewildered by her aunt's behavior, she couldn't stand by and watch this act of desperation. "It's okay. I'll close them for you."

Panic faded from Maria's expression as soon as the drapes were drawn, and for a moment at least, relief replaced her usual scowl. But there was something more telling in her eyes. She looked scared. Traces of pity began to flow inside Jeannie amidst the stream of anger still present.

"Jeannie, why don't you check our room to make sure we didn't forget anything?" her mother suggested.

Jeannie was glad to have another chance to look through the bedroom in the secret hope of finding the letters her grandmother had mentioned to her. The shelf where her mother found the wedding picture seemed a logical place, but after a quick search she found nothing else of interest. She walked out of the room discouraged but still hopeful that someday she would know more about her father's side of the family.

The door to her grandmother's room was closed, but as Jeannie passed by, she felt the calling to enter one more time. Her senses were immediately flooded with fresh memories of Sophia, the sound of her voice calling her Rose, the touch of her hair when she brushed it, and the joy in her face when she saw her wedding picture.

Jeannie's eyes wandered to the cut roses in the vase beside her grandmother's bed. The spent blossom was wilted over as if bowing to the bud whose petals were now beginning to open. The parallel of seeing one rose's performance ending as the other's was beginning wasn't lost on Jeannie. Her grandmother's life was over, a performance in which there could be no encore.

"Taxi's here, Jeannie," her mother called from the living room.

Jeannie took a deep breath to capture what life may have remained of her grandmother then hurried back and picked up her suitcase. When she faced her aunt a few words managed to tumble out. "Grandma said there were some letters. If you happen to find them would you please send them to me? I need them for a class project."

Maria stiffened, and then only nodded her answer.

Jeannie didn't speak again until the taxi pulled away from the house and it was no longer in sight. "Maria is so unlike Grandma. Are we sure they're sisters?"

"I'm afraid so, but their relationship is a mystery we may never unravel." Mrs. Fedorchak looked at her daughter and hesitated. "I have something to tell you that you're not going to be happy hearing."

Jeannie's still hurting heart pounded with dread while she held her mother's eyes.

"After Maria and I left you alone with Grandma the other day, I asked her what she meant when she said she got rid of everything." Her mother's eyes shifted away then returned. "She told me she burned everything, pictures, immigration records, anything that linked them to their past. That the wedding picture survived is a miracle."

Jeannie was silent, realizing that if Aunt Maria knew about the letters, she may have turned them into ashes, too. "Why? What right did she have to destroy them?"

Her mother shook her head. "I don't know, Jeannie, but I'm so sorry."

Jeannie felt bitterness begin to seep into every crevice of her mind. It was a poison she knew she had to stop or it would give Aunt Maria another victory. Jeannie closed her eyes and went to battle with the only weapon she had, a vision of the stem of pink roses. Its thorns weren't intended to harm the beholder, but to protect the flower. It was up to her to protect her grandmother and the beauty of their memories.

"Maria was selfish not to think that it was my past she was burning, too," Jeannie said before voicing a concern that had been tugging at her. "I don't care that she's unable to attend the funeral either, but I don't like it that Grandma won't have any family there."

Mrs. Fedorchak reached over and gave Jeannie's hand a gentle squeeze. "Father Popoff assured me the service would be full of people who loved her. Do you remember what the church looks like?"

Jeannie tried to recall her grandfather's funeral, the only time she would have seen the church. "Not very well, but it seems like there were lots of gold paintings inside of it."

Her mother smiled. "You must be remembering the icons."

Jeannie frowned in return. "Icons? What are those?"

"They're paintings of holy images that are used for teaching and prayer," her mother answered, adding, "They're also believed to be windows to heaven."

Windows to heaven...Jeannie liked that. She smiled for the first time in days knowing without a doubt, every one of them had been open for her grandmother.

Chapter Nine

"Nugget!" Jeannie dropped her suitcase to wrap her arms around the wiggling bundle of golden fur waiting at the kitchen door for them. She laughed as Nugget licked every part of her face within reach.

"I missed you, too," Jeannie said while letting the familiar surroundings penetrate her senses. It felt good to be home, as comforting as slipping her feet into her favorite pink slippers.

Mrs. Fedorchak returned to the kitchen where Jeannie was still calming her excited dog. "I have some lasagna in the freezer. How does that sound for dinner?"

"Any food sounds great, but I need to take a quick run first. My legs are aching from sitting for so long on the airplane."

"Before you go, there was a message on the answering machine for you from your new cross-country coach. Mr. Trotter is it?"

Jeannie nodded. "What did he say?"

"It was about the upcoming meet this Saturday if you were back in town," her mother answered then grinned. "He sounds like a very nice coach."

Something in her mother's last comment triggered a long time curiosity of Jeannie's. She watched her mother turn the oven on before gathering the nerve to blurt out, "Why didn't you ever get married again?"

Her mother wore an expression of disbelief when she looked back at Jeannie. "Where did that question come from?"

"It's just something I've wondered about," Jeannie said, leaning against the counter. "Well...?"

Mrs. Fedorchak released a sigh when it became obvious her daughter wasn't going to give up until she had an answer. "It's simple really. I'd always heard that lightning doesn't strike twice in the same place. I figured love was no different and that I was lucky Cupid struck even once. Besides, we've been able to manage pretty well on our own, don't you think?"

"Yes, we have," Jeannie agreed, yet the wheels in her mind were already turning as she went upstairs to change clothes and then head out the front door. Jeannie felt a sudden desire to prove her mother wrong. Emma's matchmaking methods aside, if there was someone out there right for her mother, she was going to find him.

She smiled as she started her usual route that would take her down the street where she heard the music playing the time before. *Dickson Street...the place her father proposed to her mother. Wouldn't that be a coincidence if...*

Jeannie shook her head to slow down the thoughts that began racing faster than her legs, but it wasn't long before the days of not running caught up with her. She knew she had set her pace too fast, mistakenly attempting to make up for lost time. A muscle cramp and shortness of breath forced her to take a break.

While giving her body a few moments to recover, Jeannie realized the next turn would be onto Dickson Street. She started moving again, but her mind had shifted its focus from running to listening. Passing each house, she kept her ears tuned in for any sounds of music, especially those that might be coming from a stringed instrument.

The bungalow style homes varied only slightly, confusing Jeannie at first. They all seemed to have front porches with similar stone pillars. As soon as she saw the brown ones, however, she was confident it was the right house. She paused, hoping to hear something. This time it was quiet.

Jeannie returned home with a disappointment she didn't fully comprehend. Maybe it was because she wanted to reassure herself that her ears hadn't deceived her, that she hadn't somehow imagined the music.

She headed upstairs after dinner to finish unpacking, intending to go to bed early. Jeannie knew her alarm would be going off for school at the same time it always did with no sympathy for what she had been through or how tired she was. She opened the closet door to hang up the last few items from her suitcase when a shoebox on the shelf above drew her interest.

It looked to be an older box, too small for the size of shoes she wore now. Jeannie pulled it down from the shelf and carried it to her bed, took off the lid and dumped out its contents. A rainbow of colored envelopes spread themselves on top of her sheets, some of them more faded than others.

They were cards her grandmother had sent to her through the years.

Her fingers picked a pink envelope at random and traced the handwriting spelling Jeanette. Grandma Sophia hadn't learned how to write her letters very well, but Jeannie could sense the pride in their careful formation. She pulled out the card and read its message. This one had been sent for her tenth birthday, showing a girl posed as a princess with the number 10 shaped by sparkling gemstones in her crown. It made her smile, remembering what Sophia considered to be her crown. Jeannie then set it aside and picked up another envelope, a blue one this time. There was something other than its color, however, that was different. She picked up the pink envelope again and compared them side by side. It was the handwriting.

Jeannie studied the dates stamped on each one, noticing that the envelopes with the most recent years were written in more refined lettering. Her grandmother's handwriting must have improved…or had it? She looked again at the newer set of envelopes. The answer was written in each curved stroke. That handwriting was Aunt Maria's.

This was one night Jeannie refused to let her aunt dominate her thoughts. She put the cards back in the box and threw her head against her pillow. Tomorrow would be a new day, one Jeannie couldn't wait for. She would be able to start concentrating on cross country and the rest of her life once again.

Chapter Ten

Emma's mouth flew open as soon as she turned and saw Jeannie standing right behind her in the hallway. "You little sneak. You were supposed to call me when you got home."

Jeannie put her hand over her heart. "Ah, spoken like a true friend. I'll take that to mean you're glad to see me."

"Of course I'm glad to see you." Emma's tone was emphatic. "I don't know how I've gotten through these last few days without you."

"Honestly, Emma, what could possibly have happened in Perry while I was gone?" Jeannie gave her a reluctant grin.

"Well, I can't remember everything exactly, but…" Emma nudged Jeannie with her elbow, "Brent's driving a brand new pick-up…shiny, red, and four-wheel drive." The gleam in her eyes gave away just how impressed she was.

"I'm sure his daddy made him work hard for that." Jeannie responded, making no attempt to hide her sarcasm.

Emma jumped to his defense. "He does do a lot of work on the ranch."

"I'm sure he does," Jeannie appeased her before taking the opportunity to change the subject. "Have I missed much at cross-country practice?"

"Only some new inspiration," she answered, being quick to add, "And, no, I'm not talking about Jason. Coach Trotter has the whole team working harder than we ever have."

Jeannie raised an eyebrow while she studied this new serious side to her friend. "I guess I better watch my back at the meet this weekend, especially since I haven't had much of a chance to run these last few days."

Emma sucked in a loud breath, "I'm sorry, I didn't even ask you how things went with your grandmother. Is she still…"

Jeannie shook her head to answer the unfinished question.

The school's warning bell punctuated the short period of silence that followed. Emma reached over and gave her a hug. "We'll talk later, okay?"

Jeannie nodded before turning the other direction toward her first class.

She was relieved that the morning passed by quickly, and it was already time for world history. Despite Brent Phillips being in the same room with her, Jeannie was looking forward to the class.

Mr. Trotter was standing in the doorway as she approached the classroom. He smiled, but his expression changed to uncertainty before he spoke. "It's good to have you back, Miss Fedorchak. I hope you were able to spend time with your grandmother."

Jeannie looked away to fight an unexpected rise of emotions before responding. "Only a little, she died soon after we arrived."

Mr. Trotter waited for her to look back. "You have my deepest sympathy. I know she meant a great deal to you."

"Thank you," Jeannie said then turned to walk inside the room, only to see someone else had chosen to occupy her desk in her absence. There was an empty one further back, but it meant having to pass by Brent's desk on the way. She clenched her teeth together as there was no other choice.

"Hey, how about letting me show you my new wheels?" he shot out.

Though she wasn't positive that Brent was talking to her, she wasn't about to give him the satisfaction of a response just in case. In her resolve to ignore him, Jeannie's line of vision accidentally converged with Jason Butler's. She sat down in a hurry, acknowledging that nothing had been wrong with her eyesight when she first saw him at practice. Jason had truly made a grand transformation and she had a peculiar feeling it wasn't just in his appearance.

Mr. Trotter began handing out papers to be passed down each row. "These are the guidelines for the genealogy project that will be due the week after Thanksgiving. First, you'll follow the example for making a family tree that will include your immediate family, your grandparents and your great-grandparents. I would also like for you to provide photographs where possible. Then I want you to choose one family member to write about, remembering that every one of those lives has a story worth telling."

The last words bore into Jeannie's thoughts. Archeologists spent lifetimes trying to uncover mysteries about the past. She was just as determined to keep digging into her own until she discovered the stories that ran through her blood. Aunt Maria may have made it more difficult, but not impossible.

Jeannie didn't know how long her mind had strayed when she heard Mr. Trotter's voice again.

"As we continue now, some of you may be wondering what genealogy has to do with a world history class." Mr. Trotter's eyes did a quick survey of the faces looking at him. "The answer is easy since our ancestors came from all parts of this world. Our lives are like echoes of history passed from one generation to the next. Knowing your connections to the past, no matter what they are, allow you to look more clearly into the future."

Mr. Trotter then picked up another stack of papers to pass out. "This is a poem written by my great uncle that I'd like to read to you. His words not only tell a story about his life, but also a story about the world at that time." He walked over to the podium to begin:

Tossed along the tempest sea,
Carrying dreams of what will be,
I traveled to a land unknown,
Old seeds set free, not yet resown.

Home of my birth, a stranger now,
Different faces to whom to bow,
Riches ravaged, an earth stained red,
Fear, the companion to those who fled.

Becoming Rose

A compass of despair the only guide,
Solace searched for in places to hide,
Yet fate determined to let me live,
Redeemed in full with the music I give.

My heart still mourns for those I've lost,
Tears long spent by the bitter cost,
But wills of faith and hope beat strong,
Forging a destiny where I belong.

It seemed as if he were reading it to himself again before he glanced up at the clock. "You may use the remainder of class to read and take notes on Chapter Five."

Jeannie opened her book, but it was hard to keep her attention on anything but the past few days and now this poem. After class ended, she walked back to Mr. Trotter's desk where he was sitting. "I liked the poem your great uncle wrote, though it seemed pretty sad. Did you know him?"

Mr. Trotter shook his head. "No, he died before I was born. But I think he would tell you that despite the sadness in his life, his was a happy one. I plan on sharing more about him with the class soon."

He looked as if he might say more, but Jeannie didn't give him the chance. "I wanted to let you know I'll be at practice the rest of the week. I plan on competing in the meet on Saturday."

Mr. Trotter studied her with genuine concern. "I would understand if you needed to sit this one out. Are you sure?"

Jeannie nodded, determined to extinguish any doubts he might have. "I just wish that ladybug would have brought me better luck and that I would have gotten to spend more time with my grandmother."

A smile softened Mr. Trotter's face. "We aren't the authors of our luck, Miss Fedorchak. In time, you may discover she brought you much more than you realize."

Chapter Eleven

Saturday morning, the cross country field shimmered as if a band of nighttime fairies had sprinkled glitter dust over each blade of grass. Jeannie knew the image was nothing more than the creation of sunlight reflecting off the dew, but there was a feeling of magic under her feet. Despite only being able to attend a few practices, this was the first meet of the season, and she was excited.

Jeannie was also thankful to be running on her home field, one she felt like she could run blindfolded. Her grandmother's death still lingered in her thoughts, however, making it difficult at times to stay focused. Even brushing her hair took longer as the touch of each strand took her fingers back to the feel of her grandmother's hair used to fill the pillow made for her casket.

The girl's race was about to begin, prompting Jeannie to find her favorite position in the center of the starting line. A quick glance to either side told her where the other members of her team were located, including Emma who was a few runners to the left. Jeannie gave her a thumbs-up then fixed her eyes ahead on the field.

When the loud pop sounded, Jeannie sprang forward into a swell of multicolored jerseys. She knew she had to stay toward the front of the pack if she was to have any chance of placing, so she pushed her legs into a longer stride to keep up. As usual, Jeannie saw Emma shoot ahead of her with a fast start. It produced a brief smile knowing they would meet up soon.

"Go, Jeannie," could be heard from the crowd as runners fell behind, and she was able to settle into a more comfortable pace. That's when she noticed that the boys on her team were spread out along the sidelines to cheer the girls on. Jeannie knew better than to look at them and risk losing her concentration, but the desire to know whether Jason was among them was too great. Each maroon jersey she passed tugged at her eyes, and each one that didn't belong to him was oddly disappointing.

Then Jeannie heard a loud whistle followed by, "Look at her go."

The unexpected sound of Brent Phillips' deep voice created a ripple of tension through her body. Though she would have liked nothing better than to yell at him to leave her alone, Jeannie managed not to break her rhythm, pretending that she hadn't heard him. Nothing he could do or say was worth the sacrifice of air from her lungs. The aggravation from his presence was enough waste of energy.

As the course narrowed, two girls passed Jeannie in close succession, taking her by surprise. She recognized the dark braided hair and green uniform of the second girl. They had been competing against each other since her first year of running cross-country, and up to now, Jeannie had always beaten her.

Becoming Rose

The girl glanced back at her with a bold look of satisfaction as if she were thinking this was going to be her year to win.

Jeannie stepped up her speed as the distance between them increased. She was anxious to get ahead of Emma, and now this girl as well.

Just ahead was the arched gateway of willow trees that marked the halfway point and the beginning of a long and deceptively steep hill the team had nicknamed The Exterminator. Many a runner's hopes had been dashed by its difficulty, but Jeannie had trained on it for years and she was prepared.

Once through the arch, the course opened up allowing Jeannie to scout the competition ahead of her. She easily moved ahead of a few inexperienced runners already struggling for breath, and then passed the girl with the dark braids a few yards further up. Jeannie was tempted to return the look, but she was too confused that there wasn't another maroon uniform in sight. If Emma was still in this race, she should have met up with her by now. That is unless Emma was already on the downhill side.

A surge of competitive spirit drove Jeannie up the hill with uncontrolled power. She hadn't covered more than half the distance when she realized the sudden rush of adrenalin had vanished as quickly as it came, taking all of her strength with it. The faster she tried to run, the heavier her legs became. Fighting a parched throat and burning chest, all Jeannie had left was raw determination to keep her going.

At the final half-mile turn, Mr. Trotter's intruding voice forced the painful reality into her consciousness. "Hold on to it, Jeannie. You can still place."

His words rolled over her like huge boulders, crushing what will Jeannie had left. He was telling her it would be fifteenth place or nothing. As soon as she saw the green uniform pass her again, she knew. It was nothing.

An inner pride Jeannie could no longer feel provided the final push she needed to cross the finish line before stopping. That's when she realized her head was spinning and she was in immediate danger of throwing up, something she had witnessed happen to other runners, but so far had never happened to her. Jeannie grabbed a cup of water and poured it over her face, hoping to quell the sensation. She couldn't face the humiliation of getting sick on top of losing a meet she should have easily placed in, if not won.

After leaning over to collect her breath, Jeannie saw Emma a short distance away talking to Brent and two of his friends. She started to leave when Emma turned around and caught her. Jeannie's feet and heart stopped when she saw the yellow ribbon hanging from Emma's hand.

Emma didn't hesitate to run over to her. "What happened? I was so worried when you didn't catch up with me."

Jeannie only shrugged her shoulders, unable to keep her eyes from looking at the ribbon.

Emma then held it up. "Fifth place, can you believe it?"

No, I can't, Jeannie's thoughts answered first, but as if someone else were speaking, "Congratulations," spilled from her mouth instead.

"You were right after all," Emma continued. "You always told me I could do better if I worked hard and cared more."

Jeannie couldn't find the right words to respond, knowing how much she had always worked and cared, yet it hadn't made a difference for her today. Thankfully, her mother walked up and joined them so she could change the subject.

"Mom, I thought about checking on the property before I go home. It's been awhile since I've been out there."

Her mother eyes responded in a way no words could have. They told Jeannie she understood. "Ok, but don't be too long."

"I'll talk to you later." Jeannie barely glanced at Emma before the sight of Mr. Trotter and Jason heading their direction made her exit even quicker.

If there had been magic on the field that morning, it was painfully obvious it hadn't been meant for her.

Chapter Twelve

Jeannie slowed down only a little as she turned off the main road onto the gravel and dirt one that made up the entrance to their property. Her emotions were in control of the steering wheel this time, sending the car back and forth across the worn grooves leading to her destination. At least a summer of windswept heat had dried the ground hard enough to eliminate any danger of getting stuck in mud.

Once she was past the opening line of trees, Jeannie drove into the clearing and pulled up beside the old red barn. It was what had sold her father on the property, despite its rusted tin roof and crooked walls. Her mother said his optimistic nature was convinced all it needed was a fresh coat of paint and a few nails. Unfortunately, he died before that ever happened.

The ten mile journey usually helped Jeannie clear her mind of unwanted thoughts or worries, but not this time. The recurring picture of triumph on Emma's face wouldn't leave her alone. It wasn't as if she had never been beaten out of placing before, it just hadn't happened in a long time, and never by Emma.

Jeannie stepped out of the car and gazed down the fence line that stretched until it disappeared into the horizon. A sudden desire to prove her ability began to taunt her pride. One time around the perimeter of their property would be two miles. She was certain she could make it in her fastest time yet. Ignoring her still damp jersey, Jeannie looked at the watch still fastened around her wrist. With the push of a button, her legs took off with the power she was accustomed to.

Fueled by simmering frustration, the run seemed easy. By the time she realized it had been too easy, it was too late. Jeannie felt the tightening right before the quarter turn, followed by excruciating pain. Desperate, she stopped to grab her right calf in an effort to thwart the spasm locking up her muscles. She had made two big mistakes. Not only had she forgotten to drink more water, she had let a bruised ego tempt her.

Her favorite oak tree stood close enough by that Jeannie was able to hobble over and take cover underneath its small offering of shade. She sat down and leaned against its trunk, bending and flexing her leg and foot to work the muscles loose.

As the physical pain lessened, however, tears from a different pain began rolling effortlessly down an already wet surface of perspiration. Jeannie was disappointed about the race but it was much more than that. Grandma Sophia had been the last living link to her father. Jeannie felt empty and half dead herself, but then she remembered what Mr. Trotter had said about luck. She may have wished for more, but he was right. There was no better luck than for her to have reached her grandmother in time to see her and talk to her one more time.

She continued to massage her leg while looking at the view beyond the main road that paralleled their property. The landscape consisted of fresh cut hay fields dotted with large round bales, temporary monuments to the end of another summer. A few cars were traveling down the road, but it was the dark blue cab of an older model pick-up that caught Jeannie's attention. She had seen one like it at school but didn't have any idea whom it belonged to.

After a few more minutes, Jeannie wiped away what she hoped were the last of her tears and stood up to go home. Her leg was still stiff, so she gave it another long stretch before starting the walk back to the barn. Jeannie was almost there when she heard the rumble of an engine seeming closer to her than from the road. No one else ever came onto their property that she was aware of.

Jeannie hurried the rest of the way as quickly as she could and pressed herself against the barn's backside so she wouldn't be seen. She had never been afraid to be out there alone, but now her throat felt as though it was closing in, and she was having a difficult time keeping her breathing steady. The sound appeared to be heading straight toward her.

A short glance around the corner confirmed her suspicions. She saw the outline of the blue pickup through the trees, coming her way. It had to be the same one she had just seen driving down the road. Her eyes shifted to a space between the ground and a couple of rotted boards just large enough for her to squeeze under.

Jeannie hesitated for a few seconds, remembering the field mice that had ruined her plans for turning the barn into a secret playhouse when she was a little girl. Then she heard the engine shut off, followed by the creak of an opening door. Jeannie's survival instincts took over. It wasn't until she was inside the barn with her heart drumming against the dirt floor that she felt the scrape on her back. The jagged edge of one of the boards must have gotten her, but there was enough light through the roof that a hand check to the area didn't reveal any blood.

Footsteps could be heard scraping against the brittle blades of grass outside the walls, making Jeannie feel trapped and helpless. She wouldn't be able to run, and there was nowhere to go anyway. The closest home was a quarter mile on the other side of the highway. Her body began to tremble. *Please not another muscle cramp...please.*

"Jeannie."

Whoever he was, he knew her name.

"Jeannie."

This time it was louder.

The voice didn't sound threatening, helping to allay some of Jeannie's fears. She crouched into one of the stalls and peeked through a crack in one of the panels. *Jason!* No wonder she didn't recognize the voice. She had hardly heard him speak before.

Jeannie watched him walk around with his eyes sweeping the area. She was confused why he was there, but she didn't want him to leave without talking to him. The least conspicuous way out of the barn was the same way she came in, only this time she was more careful. She hurried and brushed herself off in time to catch him as he was getting back into his truck.

"Hey," she said with a wave.

Jason stepped back from the door. "Hope I didn't startle you. I saw your car in here and wanted to make sure everything was all right."

"Everything's fine. I just came out to check on the barn and the rest of the property." Jeannie did her best to sound both nonchalant and convincing.

Jason's eyebrows furrowed in question.

"I know it doesn't look like much." Jeannie glanced away, but when she looked back Jason's eyes were still on her.

"I think it looks great, but I was wondering about you," he spoke gently.

Those words were all it took for the sting of defeat to come rushing back in Jeannie's thoughts. "Pretty awful race, wasn't it?"

Jason's gaze remained fixed. "Don't be too hard on yourself. You're a great cross-country runner who just had a tough week."

Jeannie felt herself getting upset again and nodded her response.

"Well, I'll go on now as long as you're okay."

She only nodded again.

With that, Jason climbed in the cab and leaned out the window. "I've always liked this piece of property your family owns."

His words were quick to help Jeannie regain her composure. "Wait, how did you know it belonged to us?"

The transmission clunked into gear as Jason shifted the pick up into reverse and smiled. "It's always a good idea to know who your neighbors are."

Jeannie watched him drive off, sending puffs of dust and exhaust behind him. It was then that the word *neighbors* sunk in. She didn't know which to be more surprised by, the news that they were neighbors, or the fact that she and Jason Butler had just had their first, real live conversation.

Chapter Thirteen

"Looking for something, Mom?" Jeannie asked after she returned home and saw her mother in the middle of stacks of papers and boxes on the floor.

"Not really. I just decided it was a good afternoon to organize the cabinets." Her mother answered, though her attention remained fixed on the contents of an old file folder she was holding. Even once she closed it, she stared at the blank cover a moment before looking up at Jeannie. "Emma came by. She was hoping to talk to you."

Jeannie smirked. "I bet she just wanted to show me her ribbon again. Right now, I'd rather forget the meet ever happened."

Without letting her eyes drift from her daughter's face Mrs. Fedorchak continued, "Jeannie, I know you're upset about losing, but it's more often the disappointments that make us stronger. They require us to make a choice, either accept the challenge to work harder, or quit."

Quit! The word sounded so defeating. "Mom, you know how hard I practice already."

"Yes I do, but you haven't had any significant competition in a long time, especially from a best friend.

You've always been a good runner, Jeannie, but now you have to figure out how to be even better."

Jeannie's next breath released what remained of her frustration. As hard as it was to admit, Emma had beaten her fair and square. "You're right. I'm just feeling sorry for myself when I should be happy for Emma." Then, ready to change the subject, "Have you found anything interesting?"

Mrs. Fedorchak looked at the closed folder still in her hands. "Quite a few things actually," she said before extending it toward Jeannie.

Jeannie couldn't read the expression on her mother's face and accepted the folder with some hesitation. "What is this?"

"Open it and you'll see."

Jeannie's heart was full of anticipation as she lifted the cover. The blue stick figure of a person with a crooked smile seemed to jump off the paper. She then looked at the letters scribbled across the top. Though crudely formed, Jeannie knew right away the word they were meant to spell was Daddy. Her body flinched before melting to the floor next to her mother.

"I really drew this?" she said, shaking her head with disbelief.

"I believe you were about three." Jeannie's mother encouraged her on with a gentle chuckle. "The likeness gets better in the next picture. At least you gave him hair and ears."

Jeannie's eyes were reluctant to leave the blue crayoned figure, but the reward was a burst of laughter at the next portrait of her father. He did have at least ten hairs sprouting between ears that could have easily belonged to an elephant.

The laughter left as quickly as it arrived when Jeannie turned to face her mother. "Maybe today would have turned out differently if he were still here."

Her mother shrugged her shoulders. "Maybe, but remember when you were ready to take the training wheels off your bicycle? No matter how hard your father tried and wanted to keep you from falling, he couldn't. All he could do was help you back up."

Jeannie needed that memory of her father standing beside her and picking her up. A mental search back through her childhood would have to wait until later, however. She had too many other thoughts and feelings battling for her attention. "I think I'll take these pictures upstairs to look at later."

"Before you go, I did find something else you might be interested in." Jeannie's mother reached for a long narrow box and opened it. "This is only part of your father's collection."

Underneath the lid were rows of cassette tapes. Jeannie laid the folder aside and flipped through half of them before stopping. "Dad must have really liked Bach."

Mrs. Fedorchak smiled. "Bach was his favorite, but he listened to other composers, too."

Jeannie frowned. "Don't all of them sound alike anyway?"

"I think you should find out for yourself." There was a distance in her mother's answer as if she had been taken captive by this barrage of memories.

Jeannie felt like she was on the fringe of a private conversation, not wanting to take a step closer for fear of intruding. She knew all too well about the turmoil of mixed emotions that remembering could stir up.

"Then I'll take these upstairs as well." With the folder clasped in one hand and cassette box in the other, Jeannie tiptoed away, leaving her mother to continue unlocking memories.

Jeannie felt strange, almost dizzy, as she stepped inside her bedroom. She set the box of cassettes by her stereo and randomly selected one to play while she curled up on the floor next to it with a pillow. Exhaustion had mercifully numbed her body, and for the first time that day, Jeannie relaxed enough to drop off into a much needed nap.

It wasn't long before the familiar music she had heard on her run through the neighborhood began to accompany her breathing. This was the second time it had played in her dreams, seeming to defy the efforts she made to recall it when she was awake. But this time a new melody began inching its way into her awareness, one she had never heard before.

Jeannie's eyes opened as she jerked her head off her pillow. The music hadn't been a dream, it was her stereo. Jeannie stopped the cassette and grabbed the case she had taken it from. "Bach's Six Cello Suites," she read aloud.

Her finger pushed the rewind button, and within seconds the tape clicked back to the beginning. Jeannie hit play and listened to what she now recognized as Suite No. 1. The silence that followed the last chord found her breathless as if she had been racing during the entire piece.

Since her legs remained still, it had to be something else that moved; something from deep inside of her.

A chill shimmied up Jeannie's spine with the realization that this music, composed by someone hundreds of years earlier, was connecting her to her father at this very moment. Playing it had brought it to life, making her feel as if a small part of her father was still alive in her. They were both part of this music's ongoing journey through time, from its beginning into its future.

The ringing from the telephone shifted Jeannie's reflective mood to wondering who was calling. A light knock on the door and her mother's voice soon settled her curiosity. "Emma's on the phone. Are you ready to talk to her?"

Jeannie gazed at her stereo for another moment then turned it off. "I'll be right there."

Chapter Fourteen

The only phone upstairs was in her mother's bedroom. Jeannie walked in and picked up the receiver off the nightstand, pausing before she placed it next to her ear. "Hello."

"Thank heavens. I was afraid you wouldn't want to talk to me."

As much as Jeannie thought she had put the meet behind her, the sound of Emma's voice set a fresh rush of emotions in motion. Her grip on the phone tightened while she calmed herself enough to respond. "What kind of friend would I be then?"

Emma's next words gushed from her mouth. "I'm really sorry about the ribbon...I don't even want it...I kept turning around and..."

Jeannie heard the sincere regret in her best friend's voice. "Listen to me, Emma. You ran faster than I did today, and you deserve that ribbon. To be honest, it's about time you placed."

"Well, I'd rather quit cross-country than compete against you like this."

Jeannie's competitive spirit began to return. "Sorry, it's too late for that now. I've decided we're going to aim for the top two places at the state meet."

"You're not serious."

"I don't see why not if we work hard enough. You've proved now that you can do it."

Emma sighed into the receiver. "All right, I'm game if you are...anything so long as you promise you're not mad at me. And by the way, Brent wasn't supposed to be at the meet. I told him not to come."

Jeannie's eyes automatically rolled, if only for her benefit. "Maybe now that you won a ribbon and I didn't, he'll start paying more attention to you." For a brief moment Jeannie almost felt like that alone would have made her losing worth it.

Emma grunted. "I doubt it."

"He's bound to get some sense knocked into him sooner or later." Jeannie crossed her fingers in favor of sooner, though she wished Emma would just wise up and forget about him altogether.

"Well, for now I only have another wonderful evening at Perry's finest pizza restaurant to look forward to," Emma said with teasing sarcasm.

"Have fun," Jeannie laughed as she hung up the phone and went back to her room. There was only one place in Perry to get pizza, and that was The Pizza Palace. When Emma first got the job, she had been so excited to have an endless supply of pepperoni at her fingertips. Now, she could hardly bear the sight or smell of pizza.

Jeannie tried to rest again, but her mind was too awake and restless. Her eyes danced across her pale yellow walls and ceiling before coming to a stop on the world history notebook that was laying on her desk. She had nothing else to do so she may as well work on her genealogy project. Jeannie ejected the cassette from her stereo then grabbed her notebook and headed down the stairs.

As she made her way past the cabinets, Jeannie noticed that all the papers and boxes had been cleaned up and put away. She entered the kitchen looking for her mother and found her mixing something in a bowl. "Are you busy, Mom?"

Her mother barely looked up. "No, I just had a sudden craving for chocolate chip cookies."

It turned quiet while her mother measured out a cup of sugar. Jeannie didn't know a lot about her father, but she did know those were his favorite kind of cookie. That memory must have been one of many that were released from behind the cabinet's doors, inspiring her mother to want to make them.

"You won't get any argument from me. I could probably eat a dozen of them as hungry as I am right now."

"Why don't you start with a sandwich first, you haven't had much to eat today."

Jeannie found the jar of peanut butter and spread a thick layer on a slice of bread. She took one bite then didn't stop eating until it was gone; swallowing her last gulp of milk at the same time her mother finished adding the rest of the ingredients.

"I brought down my genealogy assignment. Maybe you could help me fill in all the names for my family tree while the cookies bake." Jeannie opened her history notebook to take out the guidelines Mr. Trotter had given them, when the copy of the poem he had read to the class slipped out from behind it. She reached down and picked it up off the floor. "Here's something you might be interested in reading first. It's a poem Mr. Trotter said his great uncle wrote."

Jeannie's mother placed the cookie sheet in the oven before wiping her hands on a towel and taking the paper. A couple of minutes stretched between them before she looked up with a contemplative expression on her face. "I wonder where his great uncle was from. Can you imagine fearing for your life and having to leave a home you know you may never see again?"

The question wasn't asked with the expectation of an answer. Though to herself, Jeannie easily answered no. Perry was the only home she'd ever known. She wouldn't want to be forced to leave and never be able to return.

"Your grandparents and countless others who immigrated to this country had to make many of the same sacrifices. Maybe they didn't have to worry about their safety in the same way as this gentleman, but they gave up a lot to have a chance for a better life. From the little bits and pieces of information I could put together, your grandfather never saw any of his family again, and your grandmother wasn't allowed to stay here the first time she came."

Jeannie was suddenly intrigued. "Why couldn't she stay?"

"That, I'm not sure. Sometimes your father would try to find out more, but Sophia would start shaking her head, while repeating, 'Not important… not important.' She only hinted once that her money had been stolen and she had to return to Germany until she earned enough to come back."

Her mother's face was apologetic. "I wish there was more I could tell you."

Jeannie was disappointed. She didn't know how she was ever going to learn the truth about her father's family, but she was determined to keep trying.

"I almost forgot. I want you to listen to this, Mom." Jeannie left the kitchen and walked over to the downstairs stereo. She put the cassette in its slot then pushed the play button.

Mrs. Fedorchak had followed her daughter. "What are you…"

"Shhh…" Jeannie motioned with her finger to her lips. Then she closed her eyes.

After the first piece finished, Jeannie pushed stop. "That's the same music I heard on my run. Now that I know it was a cello, I want to find out who was playing it."

"I love the music, Jeannie, but why does that matter so much to you?"

"I don't know, except that we live in Perry, and I've never heard of anyone who plays a cello, or a violin, or any stringed instrument for that matter."

The timer buzzed for the cookies to be taken out of the oven, drawing her mother back into the kitchen. "How do you know it wasn't just a recording like this one?" she raised her voice to ask.

Jeannie answered, though she doubted her mother heard her through the wall between them. "I know…I just know."

If it was true the cello was the stringed instrument most like the human voice, there was no doubt in her mind it was speaking to her.

Chapter Fifteen

The pounding grew louder and more insistent with each knock.

"I've got it, Mom," Jeannie yelled as she ran down the stairs, skipping the last two steps. She immediately recognized Emma's silhouette through the sheer panels of fabric covering the window and threw open the door. "What are you doing up this early? It's 9:00 on a Sunday morning."

Emma flashed a broad grin. "I'm ready to go. Are you coming with me?"

Jeannie's eyes narrowed with confusion, especially upon realizing that Emma was dressed like she was on her way to cross-country practice. "Where is it you're going?"

"Don't tell me you've already forgotten, especially since it was your idea. We have lots of work to do if we're going to win the state meet."

"You want to go for a run, now?"

Emma crossed her arms and tapped her foot. "You've got exactly five minutes before I change my mind."

Jeannie shook away her astonishment and rushed upstairs to change out of her pajamas. Her leg was still stiff from the cramp the day before but not enough to make up an excuse to stay home. This was a new side to Emma she didn't want to discourage.

"So, what route did you have in mind?" Jeannie asked once they finished stretching.

Emma reached in her pocket and handed a torn strip of paper to Jeannie. "We'll go to here and back. That's at least three miles."

Jeannie recognized the paper as part of an order ticket from The Pizza Palace before reading what was written on the back, "928 Oakdale. That's over by the high school. Whose address is this?"

The light in Emma's eyes danced with mischief. "Someone's named Mr. Trotter."

Jeannie glanced at the paper again. "Emma!"

When she looked back up, Emma was already ahead of her. Jeannie had to run hard to catch up. "Emma, you know I'm not a snoop."

"Of course you aren't, but I am." Emma reached up to tighten her ponytail. I've been dying to tell you that Mr. Trotter came into the restaurant last night with none other than Jason Butler and another man I'm pretty sure was Jason's father. I made them the best supreme pizza ever, if I say so myself."

Jeannie slowed into a steadier pace. "Good for you, Emma, but that doesn't explain how you got his address."

Emma stayed beside her. "It's not like it's a big secret. It was printed right on the check he handed me at the cash register."

"I still don't understand why you want to go by his house. What if he sees us?"

"Then he'll be impressed that we're training on our own. C'mon, you can't tell me you're not the least bit suspicious of him. Doesn't it seem more than just a little odd he picked Perry to move to?"

"Who have you been listening to, Emma? Then again you may be on to something. I bet he's a spy and there's some kind of top-secret grain being stored in the elevators down at the co-op." Jeannie burst into giggles.

"I'm being serious. How is it that he seems to know Jason so well if he's new to town? And even you can't deny that his looks and the way he talks don't exactly fit in here." Emma then tipped her head. "We're almost there."

Oakdale branched off to the east from the main road that ran in front of the high school. These houses were part of a newer development, each one almost identical to the other. In fact, they were so similarly constructed with little variation in color or design that Jeannie thought it would be quite possible to accidentally enter the wrong house, especially in the dark.

Though she had kept it to herself, Jeannie was as curious about Mr. Trotter as Emma was and sought to keep her concentration and pace consistent as they turned onto his street. She glanced at one mailbox and saw the large black numbers for 912. Mr. Trotter's house would be on the same side of the street with the other even numbers.

Emma pointed her finger, "There it is."

"Emma, put your hand down." Jeannie motioned to her while relying on her peripheral vision as they got closer, hoping there was no sign of Mr. Trotter. So far it didn't look like anyone was home. At least there was no car in the driveway or a front door open. In fact, there was nothing unusual about the house at all.

"This doesn't tell us anything," Emma lamented.

"What exactly did you expect walls of brick and mortar to tell you?" Jeannie quipped just as she heard a sound being carried within the breeze that lifted the loose hair away from her face. The more she heard, the more her legs slowed down until she stopped.

"What are you doing?" Emma grabbed Jeannie by the elbow to keep her moving, but Jeannie's feet were planted firmly on the pavement.

"Listen," she whispered back.

Emma cocked her ear toward the house. "What kind of music is that?"

Jeannie felt the blood drain from her face and a chill tingle down her arms. She had listened to enough of her father's old cassettes the night before to know, "It's classical music, and that's a cello playing it."

"Okay…so…?" The question in Emma's face showed how little she understood Jeannie's reaction.

"Someone inside that house is playing a real cello," Jeannie emphasized while keeping her voice lowered.

A thoughtful pause preceded Emma's next words, "So, Mr. Trotter plays the cello? I've never seen one but I suppose that does make him a little more mysterious."

Jeannie couldn't explain the feelings that overtook her senses when she heard the music and decided not to tell Emma that the real mystery was in hearing a cello played first on Dickson Street and now again in front of Mr. Trotter's house. Though she couldn't be sure, this time she thought she heard another instrument playing along with the cello.

A sudden compulsion made Jeannie take off running again at a harder and faster pace. "I need to get home," she called back.

"Why so fast? You still have plenty of time to shower and get ready for church." Emma struggled to keep up.

Jeannie was running away from the music this time more than she was from Emma, yet she managed to toss a smile behind her. "I've got to practice beating you again."

Chapter Sixteen

The shower Jeannie took did nothing to wash away the songs that kept replaying inside her head. Led by the Bach suite, all the pieces she had been listening to melded into one continuous melody. Even paying attention in church had been close to impossible as the sermon only added lines of lyrics to the notes.

Once they were home and had eaten lunch, Jeannie went to her bedroom with a load of clean laundry and turned on her radio to the local country station. She hoped with the volume up loud enough, her mind would be able to take a break from the other music seeming to serenade her every thought.

The song that immediately met her ears was one of her favorites. "…9 to 5…" Jeannie joined in, using Dolly's upbeat chorus to help her finish folding her clothes. She turned to put away an armful of socks when a framed picture on her dresser made her pause. It wasn't as if she had never seen this picture of her family before; there was a larger version hanging on the living room wall. She had just never seen one this size, more specifically in her room.

The voice continued to sing out as Jeannie placed her socks inside a drawer then lifted the frame off the dresser.

She must have studied this picture hundreds of times over the years, yet she hadn't paid much attention to it as of late. It belonged with those memories that were slipping further from reach, retreating deeper into her subconscious. Remembering what life was like with her father had become more and more challenging.

Jeannie released a long, slow breath. Maybe that's why the music was affecting her so much. Maybe the music was really an invisible thread being used to stitch that portion of her father's heart into hers so he would never be forgotten. She had felt aches in her chest so real when she heard it that it seemed almost possible.

Jeannie's fingers stroked the glass as she gazed intently from one face to another, each happy expression frozen in a momentary flash of light. One finger sought her father's chin as if it could feel the coarse stubble of a new beard, while the rest of Jeannie's focus was on her father's eyes and the clarity with which he appeared to be looking right back at her. They were the only way she had ever known them, dressed with smiling creases at their corners and in a color as warm as melted milk chocolate.

She pushed her hair behind her ears then placed the edge of the frame against the side of her face. Jeannie wanted to see if her eyes were as similar to his as she had always thought, so she leaned in close to the mirror, hoping to get a better look at them side by side.

"I see you found the picture."

In an instant, Jeannie went from juggling the picture in her hands to looking at the real life picture of her mother framed in the doorway. "Mom, you should have warned me you were standing there."

Her mother smiled. "I did, you just didn't hear me. Do you mind turning down the radio?"

Jeannie realized she had become oblivious to its blaring sound and that her mother almost had to yell. She ran over to adjust the volume but decided to turn it off instead.

Still holding the picture, Jeannie was drawn to their images once again. "Where has this been?"

"I found it when I was organizing the cabinet the other day. We had purchased smaller pictures to give as Christmas gifts, and I'd forgotten there was one left. I thought it would be nice to frame it for you."

Jeannie pulled her eyes up first and then the rest of her head to look squarely at her mother. "Do you think I look like my father?"

"So that's what you were doing." Understanding lit up her mother's face before she went on. "The answer is yes, but don't forget you have proud Scottish blood coursing through your veins as well."

"You're not disappointed I want to learn more about the Fedorchak side of the family are you?" Jeannie asked, suddenly concerned.

Her mother's smile was reassuring. "Of course not, you've grown up knee deep in MacDonalds. You need to find out more about your father's family or your curiosity will never be satisfied."

Jeannie fought off the nagging feeling of defeat. "I don't even know where to start."

"It won't be easy without Aunt Maria's cooperation, but the next best place would be the library."

"How is the library going to help?"

"You could research the history of Austria around 1900. That would be close to the year Sophia immigrated here. Or maybe you could find out what it was like for an immigrant to travel aboard a ship to America. That will at least give you a setting for her life when she was younger," her mother suggested.

Jeannie sighed with resignation. "I guess I'll start tomorrow after cross-country practice." Then remembering something she had meant to ask her mother earlier, "By the way, do you know anything about a family with the last name of Butler?"

"Butler...," she thought out loud then shook her head. "I guess I don't. What made you ask?"

Jeannie shrugged her shoulders. "No particular reason other than they have a son my age that joined the cross-country team this year, and they live on the property across the road from ours."

Her mother's eyelids dropped. "I should have known that. If I went out there more…"

Jeannie touched her mother's hand now resting on the dresser. "It's okay that you haven't, Mom."

Sometimes she forgot how difficult and lonely these years must have been for her mother. Whoever said lightning doesn't strike twice in the same place has to be wrong.

Chapter Seventeen

Jeannie finished tying a knot in her shoelaces and stood up. For the first time in their years of running together on the cross-country team, Emma was waiting on her.

"We're going to be late to practice if we don't hurry. Are you ready?" Emma's question was woven with understanding.

Jeannie's chin rose with her next breath, summoning her courage. "Ready."

After such a humiliating performance at the first track meet, Jeannie dreaded having to face the team again so soon. She felt like she had let them down as much as she had herself. At least it would be easier with Emma beside her.

She managed to keep her head up, offering a partial smile to the wandering eyes that looked their way as they approached. When Jeannie saw Jason's she sensed something different from the others. She realized she had noticed it before when he showed up on her property. His possessed a self-assurance that was both disarming and comforting. But more than that, she knew he sympathized with what she was feeling. Jeannie offered him a full smile in return.

Coach Trotter's voice drew her attention his direction as he acknowledged their arrival with a smile of his own. "Glad you could join us, girls."

The air was thick with anticipation of what he would say next. No one could have been more relieved than Jeannie when the words he began to speak had nothing to do with the past meet or its results.

Instead, Coach Trotter's words were filled with encouragement and motivation. "While I expect each of you to set personal goals, we win a meet as a team. It will be hard work, but I know we can succeed…"

Jeannie tried to continue listening, but his message was being intercepted by both her memory and her imagination. While she saw him standing in front of her, opening and closing his mouth, her mind insisted on seeing him in a chair playing the cello music that she had now heard on two different occasions.

A poke from Emma's elbow brought her back into the present. "Twice in one day! Is he serious?" Emma whispered.

"Do what twice in one day?" Jeannie whispered back.

A grin spread across Emma's face. "The extra morning runs he was just talking about."

"Oh, that." Jeannie did her best to cover the fact she had completely missed that part of Coach Trotter's speech.

"…There's a lot of talent on this team that hasn't been fully realized. I hope all of you got some rest after Saturday's meet because now it's down to business." His eyes rested briefly on Jeannie before he continued, "To the hill everyone. We're starting with incline training first."

Both Jeannie's and Emma's eyebrows were raised as they exchanged glances and started moving in that direction. *Rest!* Emma would only have been thinking about their extra run yesterday morning, but Jeannie was doubly chastising herself for her extra run on her property after the meet.

Coach Trotter gave his instructions. He would blow his whistle once to run easy, twice to run hard, in varying durations while they climbed the hill. Then they were to circle back around for another turn. The boys went first while the girls watched. Jeannie couldn't keep her eyes from straying over to Jason as the group ran according to the whistle's commands. He made the task seem easy while some of the boys were starting to struggle toward the top. He hadn't placed in the meet either, but this was his first year and Jeannie had a strong feeling that would change at the next one.

Jeannie inhaled one long deep breath as the girls lined up for their turn. While she knew it was only a drill, she was going to make sure no one overtook her this time. If anything, she would be the one doing the overtaking.

By the time the girls finished and came around, the boys were already half way up the hill again. This was the most grueling exercise she had ever done in her life. All she could think about was how she was going to get through it again.

No words, just breathing could be heard after they finally stopped. It would have taken too much energy to speak, and no one had any left to spare. Coach Trotter could, but of course, he had only been blowing a whistle.

"Good work today, team. Be thinking about which morning works best for you to start your two a days."

It wouldn't be the next morning, Jeannie was positive. After a nice, warm shower, she intended to collapse on her bed and not move another muscle until it was absolutely necessary. Her plans to go by the library after practice would have to wait. The only subject she felt like researching now was sleep.

Jeannie flipped on her right blinker as she slowed down her approach to the next intersection. Its flashing light was a welcome sight, signaling that home was only one turn and three blocks away. But as if with a will of its own, Jeannie's foot pressed on the accelerator instead, sending her in the direction of the library. She knew it was her conscience insisting that she not put off starting her research project, and it was right. Cross-country practices were only going to get harder, requiring more and more of her time. She would just hurry in and out as fast as her worn out legs would allow.

After parking her car in the small lot behind the library, Jeannie twisted the rearview mirror downward so she could see if she looked as awful as she felt. To her good fortune, a ceiling of clouds accompanied by a strong breeze had kept her face from flushing too red and her shirt from becoming too drenched with sweat. A quick brush on either side of her head and one over her ponytail should make her presentable enough.

The library was one of the oldest buildings in town. Made of buff colored brick and carved stone, Jeannie remembered sensing how special it was from the time she was old enough to go to story hour. She knew of no other place where you could borrow something then return it, only to borrow more.

When Jeannie walked in she saw Mrs. Latimer, the head librarian, behind the counter checking out books. She couldn't imagine the library without her and mused about how she used to be afraid of her. Jeannie had long since learned that Mrs. Latimer possessed the kindest of hearts, but the tone of her voice could turn sharper than the points of both her nose and chin if someone were to break the library's most sacred rule.

Once the counter was clear, Jeannie stepped up and smiled. There were a few things she could depend on never to change, Mrs. Latimer's hairstyle being one of them. She had never seen her hair fixed any other way than twisted and pinned up high on her head.

"It's good to see you, Jeannie," Mrs. Latimer greeted her then added with a hint of scolding, "It's been awhile since I've seen you in here."

"I know...I guess I've been too busy lately."

"You should never be too busy for the library," she said before looking at Jeannie's arms. "You don't have any books to check out?"

"Not yet. I need help doing research for a genealogy project."

Mrs. Latimer nodded knowingly. "Mr. Trotter's world history class I presume. I've had a few other students come in for the same reason. It turns out some families don't keep records of their ancestors."

Or they've destroyed them on purpose for their own selfish reasons, whatever those could be, thought Jeannie.

"I happen to know that most of your mother's family still resides nearby so information will be easy to come by," Mrs. Latimer added.

"Actually, I wanted to find out more about my father's family if it's possible," Jeannie said.

Mrs. Latimer's eyes softened. "I was sorry to hear about the loss of your grandmother. She came in the library once with your mother when she and your grandfather were visiting. I had a difficult time understanding her, but her smile communicated everything that her words couldn't. It was a delight to meet her."

Jeannie nodded. "I think she had that effect on everyone."

"Now, what is it I can help you find?" A change in Mrs. Latimer's voice signaled that it was time to get back to work.

"I thought I'd start with a map of where they immigrated from. I was always told they came from Austria."

"Do you know what year they came to the United States?"

"Around 1900 I believe," Jeannie answered then asked, "Does that matter?"

"It can. The borders of many countries and kingdoms have changed over the course of wars and uprisings, Austria included. Follow me and I'll show you where our books of maps are." Mrs. Latimer led Jeannie to some shelves on the opposite side of the room.

Jeannie held such respect for Mrs. Latimer. She felt as if she could ask her anything and she would know the answer, or at least where to find it. Jeannie watched her fingers pull out a large volume.

"Your grandparents came to this country before World War I which means Austria was still part of the Austro-Hungary Empire. This book should have a map of Europe at that time and start you in the right direction. I'll be at my desk if you have any more questions."

Jeannie took the book from her. "Thank you, Mrs. Latimer.

She walked around the corner to find a table and froze. Jason Butler was already sitting at one with a couple of books opened in front of him. He gave her a quick smile then shifted his attention back to his books while Jeannie sat down and opened hers to the Table of Contents. She looked through the listing until she came to one on Austria-Hungary and turned to that page.

Her eyes had a difficult time staying focused on the map she found. They were more inclined to wander toward Jason's books, curious about what he was researching. She hoped she wasn't intruding.

It was then that the growling in her stomach started. What began as a soft annoyance grew louder until no amount of pressure from her arms could silence it. Jeannie avoided looking up, embarrassed that Jason had to have heard it as well. She could tell he was writing something down and was surprised when she felt a piece of paper touch her hand.

Jeannie picked it up and read it.

Practice worked up an appetite today, didn't it?

She hoped her face wasn't turning red as she managed to smile before bending her head back down to study the map again. Jeannie gave it an honest attempt, but this time her eyes kept drifting over to the handwriting on the paper. What was it about something written by hand that seemed to hold such power? The old cards she found from her grandmother had affected her in the same way. It was almost as if a part of one's soul was imbedded in the ink that formed each word.

Jeannie glanced over to one of his books again and was able to read the binding this time. Jeannie reached in her purse for her pen and wrote below Jason's handwriting.

Ireland?

She slid the paper back to Jason feeling a bit daring and apprehensive, anticipating his answer. Jeannie watched him write and send it back.

My mother is an O'Brien

It was her turn again. *Mine's a MacDonald...proud Highland Scot*

That doesn't look like a map of the British Isles

Jeannie glanced at the pages in front of her and shook her head before continuing the exchange.

I'm researching my father's family from Austria

So that explains your last name

Jeannie looked at him and nodded. By now, she had forgotten how tired and hungry she was, but knew her mother would be expecting her home for dinner. She checked the time on her watch and closed her book.

I have to go now, but may the luck of the leprechauns be with you she wrote then slid the paper across the table for the last time and held it there for Jason to read.

He chuckled softly then looked up and said a low, "Bye."

While Jeannie's legs should have been aching with fatigue, she felt like she was floating all the way toward her car with the paper clutched in her hand. She thought about showing it to Emma, but then again maybe she wouldn't. It would stay her secret. Jeannie opened her glove box and set the paper inside. There was nothing that could have kept her from smiling all the way home.

Chapter Eighteen

By Friday night, Jeannie was nothing short of exhausted. She had gotten up early twice during the week to get in an extra run before school, not because she was eager to take Coach Trotter up on his two-a-day suggestion, but because she couldn't sleep. Lying in bed with her eyes wide open had seemed like a complete waste of time.

"I thought you had plans with Emma tonight," Mrs. Fedorchak said as she entered Jeannie's room and sat down on the edge of her daughter's bed.

Jeannie was propped up against the headboard, balancing a sketchbook with her knees.

"Emma got called into work. One of the other girls claimed she was sick, though I have a sneaking suspicion she really wasn't." She looked up from her drawing long enough to frown at her mother.

"How about calling Sara? You haven't done anything with her in a while."

"I'm fine with staying home, Mom. After the practices we had this week, I'm too tired to feel like doing anything. It's a blessing there wasn't a meet scheduled for this weekend."

"I'll leave you to rest then, but how about showing me what you're drawing, first."

Jeannie colored in a few more additions with the pencil then turned her sketchbook around to reveal the picture.

An expression of surprise crossed her mother's face. "I've never seen you draw flowers before. It's beautiful."

"Thank you. I didn't want to forget about the stem of roses I gave Grandma before she died. She loved them so much." Jeannie turned it back around to assess her work when a sudden grin broke her contemplative mood.

"What is it? Did you remember something about Sophia?"

Jeannie shook her head. "No, the roses just reminded me of a comment Emma made about Jason Butler."

"The boy you were telling me about the other day. What did she say about him?" her mother asked.

"She said he was like a flower that was finally beginning to bloom," Jeannie answered.

A perceptible pause gave way to bursts of laughter. It wasn't until they had quieted down that Jeannie noticed her mother staring at her with a broad grin of her own.

"So...is he?" she asked, giving Jeannie's leg a nudge with her elbow.

Jeannie threw her head back against the pillow and laughed again, only this time more softly. "I'll agree he's blooming nicely."

Her mother was still grinning as she shook her head. "I do believe that's the first time I've ever heard a high school boy described in that way."

"It's just a way of saying that he's grown up to be very nice looking. But there's something different about Jason than most of the other boys at school. He's quiet, but he's not shy, and he doesn't act like he has to prove anything to anybody but himself," Jeannie tried to explain. "I like that about him."

"Hmm…" Jeannie's mother looked thoughtful, "I always knew I had a smart daughter."

"Yeah, well, I haven't had a boyfriend since fourth grade either." Jeannie gave a teasing sigh.

The phone's sudden ringing made her mother spring from the bed. "I'll answer it. I've been expecting a call from Mr. Lathrop at the bank."

Jeannie was giving her picture some finishing touches when her mother returned to her doorway. "It's Emma, and she sounds very anxious to speak with you."

"All right, I'll be right there." Jeannie couldn't imagine what could be happening at The Pizza Palace that would make Emma anxious.

"Hello," Jeannie answered.

"You've got to come down here right now. I promise I'll make it worth your while…extra olives…double cheese…anything you want," rattled off the voice at the other end of the line.

"Are you okay, Emma?"

"Yes, just hurry. Oh, and bring your mom with you."

Jeannie hung up and gazed blankly at her mother who was waiting in the hallway.

"Is something wrong?" Jeannie's mother looked concerned.

"I'm not sure." Jeannie's answer was lost in a whirlwind of thought. Then as if sparked by Emma's sense of urgency, "How does pizza sound for dinner?"

Her mother shrugged her shoulders. "I don't see why not. It sounds good to me."

As soon as Jeannie and her mother pulled into the parking lot, Jeannie spotted the dark blue pickup that looked identical to the one Jason drove. "What is she up to?" Jeannie mumbled to herself as she parked, but it was loud enough for her mother to hear.

"I think we're about to find out." Jeannie's mother grabbed her purse and led the way into the restaurant.

No one was standing at the cash register so Jeannie looked farther back behind the counter where you could watch the pizzas being made. Emma was nowhere to be seen. Jeannie then glanced into the seating area. Friday evenings were the restaurant's busiest time, but there were still a few empty booths and tables where they could go and sit down. She started walking toward a table by the window and had just passed the salad bar when she saw her. Emma was taking an order at the booth right around the corner.

If Jeannie could have performed a disappearing act, she would have, but it was too late. She and her mother had already been seen.

"Jeannie...Mrs. Fedorchak...You didn't tell me you were coming in tonight." Emma did her best to sound surprised, but she was biting her lip. Emma always bit her lip when she was up to something.

"Oh, we just happened to be hungry for pizza. No one makes them as good as you do, Emma." Jeannie's words dripped with sweetened sarcasm, but the glare in her eyes caused Emma to turn back toward Mr. Trotter who had risen to his feet.

"I'll get started on your order," Emma said, answering Jeannie's glare with a mischievous smile as she left.

"Miss Fedorchak," he said, looking first to Jeannie and then to her mother, "Hi, I'm James Trotter, Jeannie's cross-country coach."

Jeannie's mother extended her hand. "I've heard a lot about you."

"All good things I hope." There was a pause, almost a momentary lapse in time before he turned aside and continued. "Do you know Paul Butler and his son, Jason?"

"No, I haven't had the pleasure. It's nice to meet you." Jeannie's mother nodded toward each of them. I understand you have property across the road from ours."

"It's not ours yet, but we hope it will be soon," Jason clarified.

"Unfortunately, the current owner doesn't want to honor the original agreement we had with his father. We haven't given up, though," Mr. Butler added with a nod to his son.

"I'm sorry to hear that," Jeannie's mother said.

Jeannie let her eyes drift in Jason's direction feeling the pang of wanting to say something, but not knowing what. Thankfully, Mr. Trotter's voice filled the void for her.

"Would you like to join us? We've ordered much more pizza than we should be allowed to eat."

Mrs. Fedorchak exchanged glances with Jeannie before she spoke. "Are you sure?"

"Please," Mr. Trotter said, gesturing toward the booth where Jason and his father had already made room for them to sit down.

Jeannie's mother slid in first and sat next to Mr. Butler. "Paul, I feel I owe your family an apology, first for just now meeting you and second for the poor condition you must think our property is in. After my husband passed away, I couldn't bring myself to maintain it like we should have. But knowing how much Jeannie loved it, I couldn't sell it either."

"It's a fine piece of property Mrs. Fedorchak. Jason and I would be happy to help you fix it up. A little fence mending and brush clearing should take care of most of it."

"You haven't seen the barn," Jeannie joked, catching Jason's gaze, knowing that he had at least seen part of it.

Jeannie's mother's face brightened. "If you're serious, I'd like to take you up on your offer. That is as long as you call me Laura and let me pay you for your work."

"Only for the supplies, Laura, and if you'll agree to try a piece of my wife's chocolate cake, you've got a deal," he agreed.

A round of laughter lengthened into an hour of eating and telling stories. Jeannie didn't have to look at her mother to know what a good time she was having. And though she wasn't about to tell Emma, she was, too.

"I guess it's time we should call it a night. Thank you all for sharing your pizza with us." Jeannie's mother smiled then followed Jeannie out of the booth. "When would be a good time for you to take a look at the property, Paul?"

Mr. Butler looked at Jason before answering, "How about Sunday afternoon at 3:00? I always say the sooner, the better."

"Sunday would be great," Mrs. Fedorchak answered. "We'll see you then."

After saying their good-byes, Jeannie and her mother left the restaurant and started walking to the car. The outside air that met them was cooler than it had been; a sign that fall wasn't too far away and that cross-country practices would soon be more tolerable. Jeannie didn't see Emma on the way out, but figured that was probably on purpose.

Her mother was unusually quiet until they were almost home. "I'm glad we went tonight. At least now I know what prompted Emma's comment," she added in a more thoughtful manner.

Jeannie tried to recall what Emma said while they were in the restaurant. "Which comment was that?"

Jeannie's mother could no longer contain her mock seriousness and began laughing. "I'd say that, tonight, you ate pizza across from a flower just right for the picking."

Chapter Nineteen

Jeannie knew exactly where to find Emma the next day. She would be where she usually was on a Saturday afternoon, at the One Stop Beauty Shop. Owned and operated by Emma's mother, it was the only full-service hair salon in town. Offering the Saturday special of a free manicure with every haircut meant that if Emma wasn't running in a cross-country meet, she was busy painting fingernails.

Aside from the strong odors of perm solution and hairspray, there was something comforting about stepping inside the salon. It felt like home, and it had been much too long since she had paid a visit.

Emma's mother was working at the chair closest to the door when she walked in. "Is that really you Jeannie or have these fumes finally gotten to my eyes?"

Jeannie smiled, "It's really me, Mrs. Spencer."

"Well, it's mighty fine to see you. Have a seat and make yourself comfortable. Emma Lynn should be taking a break in just a minute."

This was one time Jeannie was glad she didn't have a middle name or Mrs. Spencer would have said hers aloud, too. Emma's mother held the strong opinion that there was no reason to have one if you didn't use it.

Jeannie sat down on the pink vinyl sofa, thinking how easy it was to forget Emma was adopted. She and her mother had so many of the same mannerisms and looked as much alike as any other family Jeannie knew. Jeannie hadn't asked Emma how she felt about the genealogy assignment, but doubted she had thought twice about it. Her family had always been just that, adopted or not.

For a while Jeannie was content enough to look around, marveling at how the combing and curling never stopped. Neither did the chatter for that matter. It made Jeannie wonder what it was about a chair and a hairdresser that made even the most reluctant hearts and mouths open up. While the local paper did a good job of printing the news, the most current gossip could be heard right here.

Emma was still with her customer at the back table so Jeannie picked up a book of different hairstyles to browse through. It was obvious from the cover where Mrs. Spencer had gotten the idea for her latest layered cut. If there was a record or the number of times someone changed hairstyles, Jeannie was convinced she would hold the title.

As more minutes passed, Jeannie grew more convinced that Emma was prolonging the manicure, proof that she was feeling at least a little guilty about the previous night. Emma knew she was waiting for her. She had looked up and waved when Jeannie walked in. But it wasn't until Jeannie's patience had been tested by the turning of every page that the customer finally left the table. Jeannie walked over to where Emma sat, expecting to hear an apologetic confession.

With only a slight acknowledgement in Jeannie's direction, Emma instead said, "You're welcome."

Jeannie's reply was delayed by a moment of confusion, "But I didn't say, 'Thank you.'"

This time Emma swiveled around in her chair to reveal all the self-satisfaction her face could create, "Oh, but you will."

The frown on Jeannie's face grew more pronounced. "Emma, you're not making any sense. I thought *you* were interested in Jason. Every time you see him at cross-country practice you breathe a heavy sigh and remark about how good looking he is and…"

Emma's hand flew up to stop her. "You're right, but it's not working. As hard as I've tried to like other boys, I can't keep my mind off of Brent. I'm afraid I'm destined to suffer a life of unrequited love."

Jeannie suddenly understood. "I see, so you decided I should have Jason as a boyfriend instead. That's what you were trying to stir up last night?"

"You know me. When I see all the makings for a perfect brew of love, I can't resist," she answered with a wink.

"Emma, your matchmaking notions have me worried."

"There's no need for you to worry, but I'll make you a deal. I'll agree to give up my notions once and for all if you can stare me in the eye and tell me you have no interest in Jason Butler, not now, not ever.

Jeannie threw her a look of skepticism, "Promise?"

Emma placed her hand on her chest. "Cross my heart if I should fail, then I shall kiss a slimy snail."

Jeannie laughed before returning to meet Emma's gaze, eye to eye. "Okay, you're on."

This would be easy. She had won every staring contest she ever had with Emma. Even if she did have an interest in Jason, it was worth pretending she didn't in order to win the deal. Jeannie opened her mouth, ready to deny her feelings, when images from the night before flashed through her thoughts. Jeannie's concentration drifted away, along with her eyes.

"Hah! I knew it," Emma said, reveling in her victory.

"Emma, please stay out of it. Jason and I are just getting to be friends," Jeannie pleaded. "But now I need to know why you wanted my mother to come, too."

Emma shrugged her shoulders. "Why not double the jackpot. Your mom is single. Mr. Trotter is single. And there doesn't seem to be much difference in their ages."

"Emma, that's going too far. In the future, please leave my mother out of your schemes. Besides, how are you so certain Mr. Trotter isn't already married?"

Emma's eyes widened as if she couldn't believe what she had just heard. "First of all, he doesn't wear a wedding band, and second, unless his wife never leaves the house, someone in this town would know who she was."

When Jeannie didn't immediately respond Emma continued. "Look, I was just trying to help. You'll be going off to college soon, and your mom will be all alone. Don't you think she deserves some happiness?"

Jeannie felt her defenses arm themselves. "She is happy, just the way things are. We've never needed anyone else before, and we sure don't need anyone else now."

The harshness of her own tone took even Jeannie by surprise. Some of the customers sitting close by had stopped talking and turned their heads towards them. The silence became so overwhelming that all Jeannie could think to do was get away from it. She ran out of the salon and got into her car.

Jeannie drove around town trying to stop the flow of tears that quickly followed, perplexed as to why she reacted so strongly. Of course she wanted her mother to find love again, despite her mother's claims that lightening didn't strike in the same place twice. Maybe she wanted to be the one to help find the right person, not Emma. Or maybe she was having second thoughts about interfering at all. What if her father was the only man her mother was supposed to love?

Once she was sure her tears had stopped, Jeannie went home. There weren't any tasks, however, that she could stay focused on. She didn't feel like going for a run, taking Nugget for a walk, or especially, doing homework. The hours passed by slowly until Jeannie looked at the clock and realized Emma would be at work at the Pizza Palace now. She knew she wouldn't feel better until she apologized.

Emma was behind the counter rolling out pizza dough when Jeannie entered the restaurant. For a second, she didn't think Emma had seen her come in.

"Do you need someone to take your order?" Emma asked curtly.

Jeannie breathed out a sigh. "I'm afraid what I need isn't on the menu."

"You might look again. We've added a few more items."

Jeannie had never heard Emma speak to her with such indifference. "What I need Emma, is forgiveness."

Emma threw Jeannie a hard glance before returning her attention back to the dough. "You're right. It isn't on the menu."

Jeannie knew Emma to be stubborn at times and waited for her to have a change of heart. When she continued to ignore her, Jeannie gave up and turned to leave. She didn't feel like causing any more scenes today. Once was more than enough.

"Meet you at the back table in five."

The words washed over Jeannie from behind, causing her to pause. She assumed they meant that Emma would be taking a break in five minutes but wasn't about to ask. There were only two chairs at the back table. She sat down in one not realizing how clear a view it gave her of the booth she and her mother had sat in with Mr. Trotter, Jason, and Mr. Butler. Jeannie could almost hear their conversations again accompanied by her mother's easy laughter. It had been nice to see her having such a good time. How could anyone think she didn't want her mother to be happy?

The picture of Jason's face as he sat across from her came to mind, only to be disrupted by Emma's arrival. Her arms were crossed as she sat down.

Jeannie looked at her. "Emma, you're the best friend a person could have, and I'm really sorry about what happened this afternoon. I think I panicked, suddenly afraid I was betraying my father. I do want my mother to find someone, but only if she wants to."

The edges of Emma's face grew more relaxed. "You can be such a blockhead."

"Does that mean I'm forgiven?" Jeannie dared to ask.

Emma hesitated, looking back at Jeannie. Her lips held firm, and then she popped a smile. "I guess it's on the menu after all."

Chapter Twenty

"Are you ready to go, Mom?" Jeannie hollered as she came down the stairs and into the living room. She was surprised to find her mother sitting on the sofa wedged between stacks of file folders. It was almost 2:00 and she didn't appear close to being ready to go anywhere.

Mrs. Fedorchak removed the glasses she wore for reading and rubbed the corners of her eyes. "Is it time to leave for the property already?"

"It's still a little early, but I thought you might want to get there before the Butlers do and have a look around." Then turning her attention to the files Jeannie asked, "What are all those for anyway?"

Her mother wasn't able to stifle a yawn before answering. "These are old loan applications and lease agreements I need to study for work. It's taking a lot longer than I expected."

"I don't remember you ever bringing work home," Jeannie tried to recall.

"I haven't, but keep your fingers crossed it will be worth it," her mother said, demonstrating with her own.

Jeannie wasn't sure what her mother meant, but the tiredness in her voice was unmistakable. "We could meet

Jason and his father at another time if you don't feel like going today?"

"The Butlers made us such a kind offer, that it doesn't feel right putting them off until later. Would it be awful if you went ahead without me?"

Jeannie shook her head. "I'm sure they'll understand, Mom."

Within minutes Jeannie was on the highway, heading toward their property. She was glad it was only 2:30 when she pulled in, giving her a little time until Jason and his father were to be there. One sneeze followed by another informed Jeannie something else had already arrived, billions of grains of ragweed pollen.

Jeannie had only walked as far as the small incline on the opposite side of the barn when she heard the distinct sound of tires rolling over the gravel on their road. She figured they must have seen her turn in and decided to come over early. Jeannie heard a door close right before she came around the barn to greet them.

The expectant smile she wore instantly disappeared. "What are you doing here?"

"I'm just paying my neighbors a friendly visit."

"Then you must be lost because you're mistaken if you think we're neighbors."

"Jeannie...Jeannie," Brent shook his head, "for having lived in Perry all your life, you don't know too much about what goes on around here."

Jeannie fought to keep Brent's words from crawling underneath her skin. "I know all I need to know, and I know we will never be neighbors."

"See that property across the road," Brent nodded in that direction. "We own it."

I should have known screamed Jeannie's thoughts as she held fast to her composure. "What you really mean is your father owns it."

Brent gave a shrug of complete indifference. "For now maybe, but someday it will all belong to me."

Jeannie's chest heaved with growing annoyance as her eyes shifted in the direction of Jason's home. "That property across the road is where the Butlers live. I heard they had an agreement with your grandfather to buy it."

"That's right. I forgot you've been getting kind of cozy with them. It's a real shame they don't have anything to prove it," he punctuated with chilling insincerity.

Jeannie became indignant. "What's the real reason you're here? You already know I don't want anything to do with you."

Brent didn't appear to be deterred. "I came out here to see if I could change your mind. It seems your mother is up for a promotion at the bank, and it just so happens I'm looking for a date to the rodeo banquet."

Jeannie thought she was prepared for anything, but bribery wasn't one of them. Boring her eyes deep into his, she held her voice steady, "You're an even bigger jerk than I thought. I suggest you leave now. You're trespassing on private property."

She drew a silent breath of relief as she heard the sound of another vehicle driving up. Within a few seconds Jason's blue truck had pulled up alongside Jeannie's and parked. Jeannie could almost see the taut emotions between them when Jason and his dad stepped out. The jaws of both were locked firmly in place.

"Well, I don't want to keep you all from whatever it is you're doing." Brent started to leave then jutted his chin toward Jeannie. "You might want to think about what I said."

Jeannie refused to give him a response. Once he was gone, she apologized, "I'm sorry, I had no idea he was going to show up."

"Don't worry. We do our best to ignore him." Mr. Butler's eyes suddenly looked around "Is your mother not with you?"

Jeannie shook her head. "I hope you don't mind. She had extra work she needed to have done by tomorrow." The last few words of her sentence came out more slowly as Jeannie's mind started piecing things together. The promotion Brent was talking about. That must be the reason her mother was studying those files. *How dare him* her thoughts started fuming again.

"Is everything all right, Jeannie?"

The sound of her name spoken with Jason's voice elicited a much different feeling inside Jeannie than when it came from Brent. The switch was enough to snap her away from the unpleasant situation for now. "Yes, everything's fine," she smiled. "Why don't we start inspecting the fence line first?"

The three of them walked until they had reached Jeannie's favorite tree. "I've spent a lot of time under these branches," she told them.

Jason reached out and touched an area that was missing some bark. "I hope not ever in a storm. This one's been struck by lightning."

Jeannie's eyes followed Jason's hand to what resembled a long scar in the wood. For all the times she had leaned against its trunk or sat in its shade, she never noticed it before. "I'm glad it survived."

"It's actually survived more than once," Mr. Butler joined in.

Jeannie snapped around to see where Mr. Butler was pointing to at the end of one of the branches. "You mean lightning can strike the same tree twice?"

Mr. Butler looked at her and smiled. "Especially oak trees like this one. They're struck by lightning more often than any other kind of tree."

Jeannie studied each area more closely before musing, "I wonder why."

"If I remember our eighth grade mythology, the ancient Greeks would claim it was Zeus's doing," Jason said.

"Zeus," Jeannie repeated then smiled at Jason. "Your right, he was the god of thunder and lightning."

Jason looked ready to say more when his father interrupted. "We better keep moving if we're going to get the rest of the property inspected."

Jeannie followed along while Jason and his father talked and took notes. She heard most of what they were saying, but her mind was elsewhere. Her mother had been wrong about lightning striking twice in the same place, so she might be just as wrong about love striking twice. Jeannie glanced back at the tall oak. Maybe someday her mother and her favorite tree would have something in common.

By the time Jeannie returned home, her mother was sound asleep on the sofa. She still looked tired even with her eyes closed. Jeannie tip-toed across the room and started up the stairs, trying not to awaken her.

"Jeannie?" called out a voice heavy with grogginess. "What are you doing home so soon?"

Jeannie turned and grinned. "Mom, I've been gone for over two hours."

Mrs. Fedorchak sat up with a start, causing some of the files to fall from her lap. "It can't be that late. I still have so much reading to do."

Jeannie helped pick the folders off the floor, and then cleared a space to sit down next to her mother. "Does all this have to do with the promotion you're up for?"

Wrinkles creased the space between her mother's eyebrows as she stared at her daughter. "How did you know about the promotion?"

Jeannie would have preferred not to speak the name of her unexpected visitor, but she didn't have a choice. "I saw Brent Phillips today and he happened to mention it. Why hadn't you told me?"

"I was going to tomorrow after my meeting with Mr. Lathrop. I'm not sure I even have a chance of getting it, but I certainly won't have one if I don't finish reading these," she emphasized with a sweep of her hand over the files in front of her. A finger then came to rest on her chin. "I wonder how Brent knew about it."

Jeannie skirted her emotions around his earlier attempt to bribe her. "I'm sure you haven't forgotten that Brent's dad is on the board of directors."

Mrs. Fedorchak tilted her head. "Of course not, but it still doesn't make sense that his son would know or care about what was going on at the bank."

Jeannie sensed an urgent need to change the subject before her anger resurfaced. But the next subject was just as infuriating. "I found out who Jason's family leases their property from."

Jeannie's mother set her hand on a file that had been separated from the rest of the piles. "So do, I. While these loan applications aren't current, they're still confidential. Otherwise, I would let you read this one."

"Can't you tell me anything it says?" Jeannie's expression turned hopeful.

Her mother's fingertips drummed hard against the manila covering. "I can only tell you that it raises some interesting questions."

A picture of Brent's arrogant smile flashed in front of her. "I'm sick of the Phillips acting like they own this town." Jeannie's eyes narrowed as her emotions picked up steam and she continued, "One of these days their little kingdom is going to come crashing down, and I can't wait to be there when it does."

Mrs. Fedorchak looked taken aback. "Those are strong words for not even knowing what's in this file. Is there another reason you're so upset?"

The last thing her mother needed to be concerned about was Brent's grand delusion of power. In a quick moment she regained control of her feelings. "No, it's just that the

Butlers deserve to have their own property, and I know how much you deserve a promotion. There's not another employee in that bank who's more qualified."

"I appreciate your support, Jeannie, and you're right about the Butlers. They should have a farming operation all their own by now." Her mother then straightened up. "How bad a shape did Jason and his father think our property was in?"

"Not as bad as you might think. Mr. Butler said he would have an itemized list of costs to you by the end of the week. The best news…" Jeannie paused for effect, "is that there's not as much repair needed to the barn as we thought."

Mrs. Fedorchak's entire face brightened. "I know how happy that would make your father."

"By the way, I learned something else while we were out on the property." Jeannie then stood up from the sofa and stretched. "And you're entirely mistaken, Mrs. Fedorchak."

"And just what is it I'm entirely mistaken about, Miss Fedorchak?" Her mother seemed to sense the game.

Jeannie only answered with a sly grin and ran up the stairs.

Chapter Twenty-one

The results from the next cross-country meets were proof that Mr. Trotter's training methods were working. Though they seemed brutal at times, Jeannie already felt like a better runner because of them. Best of all, the girl in the green uniform and dark braids had yet to pass her again.

She and Emma were both in high enough standing to be strong contenders for the upcoming state meet, but Jeannie was careful not to become over confident. Not a day passed when she didn't think about training, at least until this morning. She was restless, but this time it didn't stem from the urgency to run. Jeannie was nervous and wanted to know if her mother had found out any more about the promotion at the bank.

Mrs. Fedorchak was curled up in the old leather arm chair reading a book when Jeannie found her in the living room. Without a second's warning, however, Jeannie's mind swapped reality with a vivid memory. Instead of her mother, it was her father sitting in the chair with a newspaper spread open between both hands. Jeannie stood motionless as she watched him lift his head and look at her. She held her eyes glued to his as long as she could, aware that in another blink, he would be gone.

Her mother's voice prematurely dispelled the vision from Jeannie's past. "I hope you don't mind that I borrowed your father's cassettes from your room."

Jeannie hadn't noticed the music playing until then and smiled. Maybe it was the pairing of the leather chair and the music that had created the image of her father, though for a moment it seemed as real as anything else her eyes had ever seen.

"Of course not, it's just good to know I'm not hearing things, too," she said, mumbling the last few words as she sat down in a chair across from her mother.

Jeannie's mother placed a bookmark between the pages and looked up. "Is everything okay?"

Jeannie tried her best to keep the concern out of her voice. "I was just wondering if you had heard anything about the promotion yet."

Her mother shook her head. "The final decision is up to the Board of Directors and they don't meet again until next week. You're not worried are you?"

"No, but if for some reason they don't promote you, I think you should find a new place to work."

"Jeannie, I admit I'll be a little disappointed if I don't get it, but I'll be fine. It's only a job."

Jeannie gave her mother a more intense look. "I just want you to be happy."

"I am happy." This time her mother's words were coupled with a curious frown. "Are you sure everything is okay?" she asked again.

Jeannie nodded, trying to assure both her mother and herself. She had said she wasn't worried, but she was. What if Brent really did have the power to influence the board's decision? Jeannie knew she needed something to distract her mind for a while. "I think I'll go out to the property to see how the repairs are coming? Jason said he and his dad would be working this afternoon."

Her mother's eyes turned toward the window. "It still seems nice enough outside for now, but I heard there's a cold front moving in. The forecast is predicting a chance of storms."

"Mom, you know the weatherman is wrong more often than he is right. But I promise I'll keep an eye on the sky just in case."

"Just not while you're driving," her mother teased with a smile.

Jeannie stepped outside to go to her car and glanced up to see an ocean of blue sky, not a current of clouds in sight. *A cold front, huh,* she thought. She started to open her door when something lodged in the windshield wiper diverted her attention.

Her first thought was that a piece of trash had simply gotten trapped there by a strong gust of wind. Jeannie reached over to free it when she saw the letter *J* followed by the rest of the letters that spelled her name. Anger sped from her eyes to her fingertips as she read the words written underneath…*Time is running out.*

Jeannie couldn't crumple the paper fast enough before tossing it to the ground and kicking it away. She was trembling as she started the car and backed out of the driveway, intent on going to Brent's first and telling him once and for all that his game was over. It would be the last day of never before she would ever go out with him.

The closer she got to the highway, however, the more Jeannie realized she couldn't just show up at his house. Her fist came down on her steering wheel as she pulled to the side of the road and stopped. Nothing would feed his ego more than to know how she was reacting right now. After a few calming breaths she turned the car around and drove back the other direction, determined that Brent wasn't going to ruin the rest of her afternoon.

Thoughts of seeing Jason and his dad helped Jeannie renew her focus for the remaining distance to the property. Within a few more minutes she was pulling up beside Jason's pickup and a newer model brown one she assumed belonged to his dad, parked close to the barn. Neither of them was in sight when she stepped out of her car, but what she did see was hard to believe. The overgrown brush had been cleared and several trees trimmed of their dead branches. They had already done so much work when Jeannie knew they had plenty to do on their own property.

The revving sounds of a chainsaw drew Jeannie down the path to a small stand of trees at the northeast corner of the field. It was there where she found Jason cutting and stacking logs from a fallen tree, no doubt a victim of last winter's ice storm. Realizing he must not have heard her walking up behind him, Jeannie stayed quiet as she watched him pause to wipe his forehead with a bandana he pulled from his pocket. She may have remained unnoticed had a sneeze not escaped and given her away. Jason's head snapped around and he shut off the motor.

"It's the ragweed," Jeannie explained before sneezing again.

"God bless you," he said, his expression melting into an immediate smile. "I'm sure this dust isn't helping either, but at least you won't be running out of firewood anytime soon," he said, nodding his head toward a much larger pile of cut logs.

Jeannie took in its size. "You can say that again."

Jason's smile broadened. "Don't worry. We'll haul it to your house and stack it for you."

The sight of the brown pickup driving across the field toward them diverted their attention. Jeannie could see that it was Mr. Butler waving his arm out the window. They waited quietly until he drove up beside them. "I'm glad you came out today, Jeannie. What do you think?"

Jeannie grinned. "I hardly know what to say, Mr. Butler. I've never seen this place looking as nice as it does now."

"I hope your mother agrees with you."

"Believe me, she will."

Mr. Butler's eyes shifted to Jason. "I need to make a quick trip into town. You should probably finish up for the day. The wind has shifted, and it looks like the front they predicted is about here."

Both Jeannie's and Jason's faces rose to the sky. It seemed the weathermen were right after all. The sun looked as if it had only a short time left before it would be swallowed up by the mouth of a giant dark cloud.

Jason turned toward Jeannie. "Let me get my tools, and I'll walk back to the barn with you."

The sky grew darker with each moment she waited, yet Jeannie didn't feel the need to hurry. It wasn't until they were on their way back to the barn that the winds began to increase and a bolt of lightning flashed in the distance, followed seconds later with the low rumble of what sounded to be a hungry sky.

"We better make a run for it," Jason said, picking up his step.

They hadn't gotten but a few strides farther when the sky opened up and it began to pour.

"On second thought, I'll race you," he challenged.

The last thing Jeannie anticipated doing today was running, especially in a thunderstorm. Even without the rain and a head start, Jason would have beaten her. He was already faster than she was when he joined the cross-country team, and he had improved a great deal since then. It didn't make her feel any better that he was also carrying a chainsaw and a bag of heavy tools.

When she caught up with him at the barn, he had the door unlatched and open. Another crack of thunder hurried them inside. "That one was a little too close," Jason said after closing the door.

As Jeannie's pupils adjusted to the dim light, she could see the repairs that had been made. There were no longer any large gaps in the wooden panels like the one she had crawled through before, and the sagging roof had been bolstered in place with a new support beam. "It doesn't seem as scary in here anymore. I wish my dad could see all you've done."

Jason followed Jeannie as she walked to the middle of the barn. "It didn't take that much really. After a couple coats of paint, she'll be about as good as new."

Jeannie's eyes continued to scan over every surface before coming to rest on Jason's. "That was an unfair race by the way."

"Yeah, I know." He broke into a grin.

If this had been a staring contest, Jeannie would have lost. She looked down to get away from the eyes she was afraid could penetrate every one of her thoughts. For what felt like an eternity, the only sound between them was the raindrops beating down against the metal. Yet she sensed he was still looking at her.

"May I ask you something?" Jason's voice sounded hesitant.

Jeannie raised her head back up. "Sure, go ahead."

He paused a moment before he started. "How old were you when your father died?"

It wasn't a question Jeannie expected, but she was glad he felt comfortable in asking her. "I was only five," she answered.

Sympathy infused Jason's face. "That must have been hard on you and your mother."

"It was, but sometimes I feel like it's gotten harder, the older I get. I was hoping to learn more about his side of the family for the genealogy project, but the only member left is a crotchety old aunt who has been no help at all," Jeannie responded, but wanting to make sure they didn't start talking about Aunt Maria, she quickly changed the subject.

"Now it's my turn to ask you something," she posed with a smile. "Why did you wait until your senior year to join the cross-country team when you were obviously good enough, and how is it you seemed to already know Mr.

Trotter?" She didn't mean to end with a shiver but a chill from being wet had settled in.

"That's two questions, now," Jason teased. "Why don't I explain some place where it's warm and dry and where you can call your mom to let her know you're all right. It's a place that also has the best chocolate cake you'll ever taste."

"I don't think the training manual Mr. Trotter gave us recommends eating chocolate cake."

"Then I must have a different version. Mine says right on the first page that to be the best cross-country runner, you must first eat a piece of Mona Butler's chocolate cake."

Jeannie laughed. "No it doesn't."

Jason shook his head. "If you don't believe me then I guess you'll have to see for yourself. Shall we make a run for my pick-up?"

Chapter Twenty-two

Jeannie had never been so sorry that a storm was over. It felt much too soon for Jason to be taking her back to the property where her car was still parked. For having been so cold and wet earlier, Jeannie felt nothing but warmth radiating inside of her now. She supposed it could be the lingering effects of the hot tea and delicious chocolate cake Mrs. Butler had served her, yet one glance at Jason confirmed the real reason. Her heart pounded with a feverishness that was different from anything she experienced during a cross-country meet.

Jason drove slowly, steering his pickup around the deep puddles of rainwater that had collected on the road. Jeannie knew he was being careful not to get stuck, though this was one time she didn't think she would mind. She stayed quiet for most of the ride back, trying to remember all the things Jason had answered about joining the team and how he met Mr. Trotter.

Once they pulled up beside her car and stopped, she turned and looked at Jason. "So Mr. Trotter came to Perry because he had a great uncle that once worked for a big ranch north of here?"

Jason flashed a grin. "Yes."

"And this ranch was famous for its Wild West show."

"Yes."

"And this great uncle was a musician who had escaped Russia and was hired to perform in this Wild West show."

This time an amused Jason just nodded his head up and down.

"So Mr. Trotter decided to visit where this ranch used to be, got a teaching job in Perry and moved all the way from New York to live in the middle of nowhere." This time Jeannie didn't wait for a response. "Do you know how crazy all of that sounds? Not to mention that he also ended up being our new coach."

If Jason considered answering the question, he gave in to laughter instead. "Well, when you put it that way."

Jeannie laughed, too, thinking the whole time how much she could never tire of hearing his. "Well, I'm glad it was you who gave Mr. Trotter directions the day he got lost and that he talked you into joining the cross-country team."

Jason gave her a long look in return. "So am I," he said letting a minute of silence pass before adding, "I'll follow you off the property to make sure you get on the highway."

Jeannie was reluctant to get out of the pickup and into her cold car but knew she needed to get home. "Thanks. I guess I'll see you tomorrow then."

Within a few minutes, she was retracing the tracks left by Jason's tires. The task would have been easier had her eyes not kept drifting to the rearview mirror just to see him behind her.

All through a shower and dinner, Jeannie couldn't stop thinking about her afternoon with Jason and his family. Mrs. Butler was as friendly as her chocolate cake, while

Jason's younger brother, Alex, was a striking reminder of what Jason used to look like. Jeannie didn't need a crystal ball to predict the transformation that would be taking place in his near future.

The dreamy replay of each moment kept a constant smile on Jeannie's face. Her feelings for Jason were such that even she couldn't deny them any longer. As hard as it was to admit, Emma had been right.

"You've been awfully happy for someone who wasn't much better off than a drowned rat this afternoon," Mrs. Fedorchak said as she took a step inside Jeannie's room later that evening.

Jeannie didn't know how else to react to her mother's comment other than to keep smiling.

Her mother lifted her chin as she took in a knowing breath, "Maybe I should ask if you even remember that it stormed today and that the temperature dropped a chilling twenty degrees."

Jeannie's mouth opened then fell closed with a sigh, "Is it that obvious?"

"Probably just to me."

"No, I'm afraid Emma already has her suspicions."

Jeannie's mother walked over to sit beside her on the bed. "Is there a reason you want to keep your feelings to yourself?"

Jeannie became more pensive. "I think it's because the thought of having a boyfriend is all so new, and I don't want to mess it up. And what if Jason doesn't feel the same way about me? That would be humiliating."

Her mother smiled. "You don't need to worry about that, I saw the way he looked at you the night we ate at The Pizza Palace. Just be patient and give it time."

"I'll try," Jeannie said then added with an enthusiastic tone, "I hope you get to meet his mother soon so you can eat a piece of her cake. It's melt in your mouth heaven."

"I hope so, too, and to thank her as well. I imagine she took great care in getting you warm and dry. But right now we should both get a good night's sleep." Jeannie's mother stood to leave.

Sleeping was the last thing Jeannie thought she would be able to do in her present state. "Before you go, Mom, I was thinking about calling Aunt Maria tomorrow to see if she would send me Grandma's wedding picture. I'd like to use it for my project."

Her mother paused before responding. "I don't think I need to warn you how she might react, but if it's that important, why wait until tomorrow to find out."

Jeannie glanced at the clock on her nightstand. "Isn't it too...," she started then caught herself. "I forgot it's two hours earlier there isn't it?"

Her mother nodded. "I think you should call her now. I have her phone number in my room."

Jeannie followed her across the hall and watched her pull a small red address book out of the nightstand drawer. Jeannie's focus went from the book to the phone sitting on top of the nightstand.

"You have to pick it up first," nudged her mother.

She placed her hand on the receiver then hesitated. "Why does Aunt Maria have to be so intimidating? And what if she decided to destroy it like she did everything else?"

"Aunt Maria can only be intimidating if you let her. You will never know what happened to the picture unless you call." Her mother then held the book open for her.

Jeannie sought to draw strength from her mother's eyes then hurried to dial the numbers before she could change her mind. By the fourth ring, Jeannie was ready to hang up. "I guess she's not..."

"Hello."

The word thwarted Jeannie's ready retreat. Her mouth opened, but no words immediately followed. "Aunt Maria, this is Jeannie," she managed to pry out.

"Hello, Jeannie."

Jeannie almost thought she had dialed the wrong number. She expected to hear a battle cry, but the voice on the other end of the line no longer sounded like the enemy. It took a moment to disarm her defenses before she spoke again. "I wanted to ask if you would mind sending me the picture from Grandma's wedding. I was hoping to use it for my genealogy project at school."

She sat down on her mother's bed while Aunt Maria answered. "No, I understand...thank you for telling me." She put the receiver back in its place.

"Well?" Jeannie's mother stopped pacing the floor and waited.

Jeannie looked at her mother and shook her head. "Aunt Maria doesn't have the picture anymore. It's with Grandma."

Mrs. Fedorchak was still while the full measure of the words was comprehended, "Jeannie, I'm so sorry."

"It's okay." Jeannie felt the weight of disappointment lift. "Grandma loved that picture and it makes me happy to know it will be with her forever. I'm just surprised how glad Aunt Maria seemed to talk to me."

"Maybe it's because she's alone now. I would think that would change someone," her mother said pulling back the covers and climbing into bed. "We'll talk more tomorrow, I promise."

"Good night, Mom. See you in the morning."

Jeannie returned to her room in a changed mood, torn between joy and melancholy. Speaking to Aunt Maria brought back bittersweet memories of seeing her grandmother for the last time. She reached over to pick up her sketchbook and looked at her almost finished picture of pink roses. The wedding picture may be gone, but at least she had this picture to remind her of their short but special time together.

She thought again about how different Aunt Maria sounded. While it had always been so easy to be angry with her, now it wasn't. Seeds of a different emotion were taking root and she found herself feeling sorry for Aunt Maria instead.

A whimper from the side of her bed stole the opportunity for any further reflection. "Don't tell me you're ready for bed, too, Nugget."

Nugget answered with another whimper.

"Come on up here then. I believe I'm exhausted after all."

Chapter Twenty-three

For days afterward, Jeannie felt as if her feet were barely touching the ground, even while she was running. A moment from the day before had only increased the buoyancy in her step, when after a quiet walk to her car Jason turned and asked, "Would you like to go out with me tomorrow night?"

The question had taken Jeannie by surprise and her cheeks still warmed with embarrassment when she recalled how her answer stumbled out of her mouth. She still couldn't believe that within a few hours she would be on her first date with Jason.

Emma was waiting outside for her after school, and they started heading toward the parking lot. "It was awfully nice for Coach Trotter to give us a day off this close to the state meet, and on a Friday no less. Have you made any plans?"

Jeannie held onto her answer until she was caught by Emma's probing eyes and couldn't contain her smile any longer. "Yes."

"You're going out with Jason, aren't you?" Emma shot her a knowing look.

Jeannie's mouth opened up but paused. "Wait, how did you know?"

Emma laughed before stating matter-of-factly, "Don't you remember, I have a sixth sense about these things."

"Oh, excuse me, I forgot about your special gift." Jeannie continued smiling as she rolled her eyes.

Emma feigned a pout. "It is special, but then anyone who has been around you two would know you belong together. Where are you going?"

Jeannie shrugged. "He just said he'd pick me up around 6:00. If we end up at the Pizza Palace will you promise to behave yourself?"

Emma's response was delayed by a formation of Canadian geese honking as they flew low overhead. Both heads tilted skyward to watch them until their wings carried them out of sight.

After their chins lowered, Emma's eyes locked onto Jeannie's. "I won't be working tonight."

Jeannie was sure Emma was kidding. "What do you mean? You work almost every weekend."

The corners of Emma's mouth remained fixed. "I'm going somewhere with Jimmy."

The words hung in the air before sweeping through Jeannie's memory. It didn't take long for her to guess where Emma was going. "You're going to the rodeo banquet, aren't you?"

By then they had reached Emma's car and stopped. "I wasn't planning on it. But then Jimmy asked me, and I felt sorry for him."

Jeannie had managed to push away any thoughts of Brent Phillips and shuddered now at their return, all because her best friend agreed to go to the banquet with Brent's best friend. It took her a moment to look at Emma again.

"I hope you're not too mad at me. I know you don't really care for Brent or any of his friends," Emma added somewhat sheepishly.

"At least I like Jimmy the best," Jeannie said, wanting to ease Emma's mind. "I hope you have a good time, and I mean it."

"I'll try," Emma sounded somewhat relieved, "but I expect a full report of your date tomorrow, in detail."

Jeannie waved goodbye then drove home, questioning Emma's real motive for going to the banquet. She doubted it had as much to do with Jimmy or his feelings as it did having an opportunity to spend time in Brent's company, even if he was with another girl. Jeannie's last thought suddenly generated a disturbing question. Who was Brent going to the banquet with if it wasn't her?

As Jeannie pulled into the driveway, she saw that her mother's car was already there. Her mother never left work early unless she was sick, and she had seemed fine that morning. Jeannie gave Nugget a quick pat, unsettled by the quiet that greeted her when she entered the house. "Mom?"

An answer of silence hastened her to the bottom of the stairs. "Mom, are you up there?"

The only sound to be heard was the pendulum of the grandfather clock clicking away each second with marching precision. Jeannie then saw her mother appear at the top of the stairs and start to descend. What met her eyes once her mother was in full view was startling. No amount of make-up could have hidden the red and swollen eyes. "Mom, what's wrong?"

Mrs. Fedorchak walked over to the sofa to sit down. "I'm just being ridiculous."

Jeannie sunk down in the cushion beside her mother. "You've never been upset over anything ridiculous. What is it?"

"Mr. Lathrop called me into his office today to tell me about the board's decision. He couldn't look me in the eye, and his hands were so fidgety, I knew right away someone else had been given the promotion." Her mother spread apart the tissue that had been clutched in her hand and blew her nose. "I told myself all along that it didn't really matter, but…"

The rest of her mother's words were muffled by the rapid flow of anger moving through Jeannie's entire being. She closed her eyes to calm herself, but the vision of a mocking Brent threw them open again.

"I must have been wrong to think I had the qualifications they were looking for."

"You weren't wrong, Mom. You should have gotten the promotion."

Jeannie fought to keep from drowning in what was now a river of overwhelming guilt. There was only one way to fix this. "I need to go up to my room for a little while. Are you going to be all right?"

Her mother nodded. "I'll be fine."

Jeannie ran up the stairs and into her mother's room first. She opened the drawer to the nightstand and pulled out the phone book. After flipping through a few pages she found what she was looking for. "Phillips," she mumbled to herself as she moved her finger down the list then stopped.

Jeannie picked up the phone and dialed. She didn't care if Brent had found another date. Four rings then five. He had to answer.

The rings stopped only to be followed by a long pause. "Hello?" Jeannie said.

"I wondered if you might call," Brent answered.

Jeannie didn't dare breathe lest her courage disappear. "If I go with you to the banquet tonight can you promise my mother will get the promotion she deserves?"

"So you're sorry now you didn't take my offer?"

"Is it a deal or not?"

There was silence before Brent answered, "Deal."

"I'll meet you at the fairgrounds. 6:00." Jeannie hung up. She may have sounded strong while she was on the phone, but now that she was off, her hands were shaking.

She went into her room and flung open her closet door. Her hands pushed aside one hanger after another until she lifted one off for further inspection. "This should do."

Jeannie held the dress of coral lace in front of her as she looked in the mirror. All she needed was a pair of her mother's heels to complete the outfit. Borrowing them was easy since they wore the same size, and her mother had never minded before.

There were several boxes of shoes in her mother's closet, but it wasn't until Jeannie opened one off the top shelf that she found the perfect pair. The shoes were cream leather pumps with a satin bow across the open toe. She thought it a little odd that she didn't remember ever seeing them on her mother's feet. They weren't brand new, but the soles looked as if they had never taken a step on hard pavement much less dirt or grass. Maybe her mother had forgotten she had them.

After applying fresh make-up, Jeannie twisted her hair up the back of her head and secured it with a gold clip, leaving a few shorter strands loose around her face. She took another glance at her reflection and left the room.

Jeannie saw that her mother was lying down resting, though the loud creak from the bottom stair changed that. Her mother's eyes opened, and she sat straight up. "Where are you going dressed like that?"

"Did you forget about the rodeo banquet tonight?" Jeannie held her jaw firm with determination as she gripped her car keys. She would have to make as little eye contact as possible if she was going to succeed in getting out the door. One long look between them and the precarious threads holding her emotions together were certain to unravel.

"I heard people talking about it at the bank today, but I thought you told me you were going out with Jason," her mother said.

Jeannie froze in midstride. In the midst of trying to fix this awful nightmare, she had forgotten to call Jason to see if she could meet him later. There was no time to respond to her mother as her next breath was cut short by the ringing of the doorbell. Jeannie had no doubt that the outline of the figure on the other side of the door was Jason's. What was she going to tell him?

"Are you going to answer it?" her mother asked when Jeannie showed no sign of movement.

Jeannie felt sick at her stomach, but she couldn't leave him waiting on the front porch any longer. She took the few steps to the door and turned the knob. The magic when her eyes met his smile was more perfect than she dreamed it could be.

Then Jason's eyes dropped to her feet and rose slowly, taking in her full appearance. His smile had disappeared. "I had no idea you would be so dressed up."

Jeannie struggled with how to ease the confusion on his face when she was so confused herself. "I'm sorry, Jason. I meant to call you before you left home and ask if you minded meeting me a little later tonight. I need to help my mother out with something."

Jason's expression relaxed a bit. "That's okay I guess. What time do you think it will be?"

Jeannie's heart was in a wretched game of tug-a-war. It wasn't too late to change her mind and go with Jason. But then what about her mom and her deal with Brent? A few moments of indecision were all it took for the nightmare to create its next scene. Jeannie watched in horror as Brent's pickup rolled up in front of her house and stopped.

Brent got out of his pick-up and started walking toward the sidewalk. He was wearing what looked to be a new pair of blue jeans and boots with a pressed white shirt to complete the look. It was obvious he thought he was going somewhere special.

"Help your mother?" Jason's words bordered contempt. "It's time for me to leave."

"Jason, wait. I don't know what he's doing here. It's not what it looks like."

His hesitation was brief as he kept his back to Jeannie. "There has never been anything wrong with my eyesight."

Chapter Twenty-four

Jeannie held her breath as she watched Jason and Brent pass within inches of each other. One wrong word or gesture was all it would take to ignite the short fuse of tension between them. After a nervous moment she was able to release the air, thankful that for once Brent kept his mouth shut.

As Jason accelerated away in his pickup, Jeannie fought back heartbreaking pangs of regret. She feared he would never want to speak to her again or worse that she had lost his trust forever. The knowledge that Brent was now standing in Jason's place on the porch made it all the more painful.

She tried to look at him, but there wasn't any part of his appearance that wasn't repulsive to her. "I told you I would meet you at the banquet."

"Now that wouldn't have been a proper date would it?" He forced his way into her line of vision before adding, "And I would have missed the pleasure of seeing Jason."

Jeannie took a step back. "Keep Jason out of this. This is between you and me and the fact that my mother should have had that promotion."

"Don't worry, after tonight it will all be fixed," Brent said, gloating with the satisfaction of an animal that had just captured its prey.

Jeannie felt her resolve slipping away when the door swung open and her mother appeared in its threshold.

"Hello, Brent."

Brent tipped his hat. "Mrs. Fedorchak."

"I didn't realize you two had made plans this evening," she said glancing from one to the other. When neither of them responded she continued, "I'm afraid Jeannie is going to have to stay home tonight. I've just received news of an urgent family matter."

Her mother was gentle yet firm as she took hold of Jeannie's shoulders to guide her back into the house. "Maybe another time, Brent."

With that Jeannie's mother closed the door, and didn't speak again until she finished leading Jeannie to the kitchen and sat her down in a chair at the table. "I don't know what just took place on our front porch, but I'm going to fix us a cup of chamomile tea while you tell me."

By then Jeannie was trembling. "Mom, I'm not even sure myself. All I know is I've made a complete mess of everything."

Her mother filled the tea kettle with water and placed it on the stove to heat. "How about starting with why you would give up the handsome prince to go out with the loathsome beast. I know how you feel about Brent Phillips, and you would never choose him unless your life depended on it or maybe someone else's you cared about."

Jeannie looked wide-eyed at her mother. It was if she already knew.

"Jeannie?"

All the anger and guilt burst into parallel streams of tears. "I didn't think Brent would go through with it and now I've hurt Jason. He's sure to hate me now."

Her mother sat down and wrapped Jeannie's hands inside hers. "Jason is a reasonable young man, and I'm sure there's a reasonable explanation for all of this. I'd like to help, but first I need to know what happened."

Jeannie looked at her mother with pressed lips, but the words couldn't be stopped. "It's my fault you didn't get the promotion."

The whistle from the tea kettle intruded long enough for Jeannie's mother to get up from the table and pour boiling water into the teapot. When she returned, her face was shaded with new concerns. "That doesn't make any sense, Jeannie. How could any of this have to do with the promotion, especially you thinking it was your fault that I didn't get it?"

Jeannie paused while she took in a slow shaky breath. "It's because I wouldn't go to the rodeo banquet with Brent. He showed up at the property the afternoon we were to meet with Jason and his dad. He tried to bribe me into going with him by telling me about the promotion you were up for. I didn't believe he could actually…"

"Stop right there, Jeannie." Her mother's eyes had narrowed. "Brent may be spoiled and used to getting his way, but if anyone kept me from getting the promotion, it was me."

Jeannie wiped the tears from her face and frowned. "Now, who's not making any sense? You were the most qualified person for the job."

"Maybe, but I've been thinking things over. Do you remember the old files I was studying for Mr. Lathrop? And there was one in particular that caught my attention?"

Jeannie's head moved up and down in response to both questions. "You said the information was still confidential."

"I showed it to Mr. Lathrop when I returned the files, and he thought it was as unusual as I did. My guess is Mr. Lathrop brought it to Mr. Phillips attention, and Mr. Phillips wasn't happy that I had found it. He may have thought the best way to keep me quiet was to keep me from getting the promotion."

"I wish you could tell me what was in it."

Her mother got up to bring the teapot and cups to the table. "I have a feeling you'll know soon enough. For now, I want you to drink your tea. There's nothing better than chamomile to calm your nerves."

"First, let me give you back your shoes." Jeannie pulled them off one at a time and set them on the table.

Astonishment filled her mother's face. "You found them."

Jeannie wasn't sure what her mother meant and began explaining, "They were up in a box in your closet. I didn't have any heels to wear and thought it would be all right to borrow them."

Her mother closed her eyes a moment. When she opened them they were accompanied by a wistful smile. She picked up the shoes and cradled them in her hands, inspecting them thoughtfully. "These are the shoes I wore at my wedding."

The last word caused Jeannie to gasp. "No wonder I've never seen them before. And to think I almost went out with Brent in them."

Mrs. Fedorchak gave her daughter a determined look. "But you didn't. From now on I want you to keep them in your closet."

Jeannie glanced at the shoes her mother had placed back in front of her. "Why?"

Her mother's laugh sweetened the room, seeming to rewind the clock to a time before the hurts and disappointments of the day. "Don't you see? I've been saving them for you."

Jeannie's face lit up with understanding. "You mean for when I get married?"

"Or any other special occasion you'd like to wear them to." Her mother winked.

Jeannie took the heels, handling them more carefully than she had before. If happy memories were the measure of something's worth, these were indeed a treasure. She carried them up the stairs to her bedroom and tucked them back inside their box.

Whatever the occasion was when she wore them again didn't matter. Jeannie would keep them safe next to the treasure equally as valuable to her, the box of cards from Grandma Sophia.

Chapter Twenty-five

When Jeannie awoke the next morning it was as if a vacuum, powered by all her emotions, had sucked every drop of life out of her. Sleep had given her a few hours of peace, but the memories were quick to return, advancing back into her consciousness to the beat of a throbbing headache. She had no motivation except to stay in bed and be miserable.

It wasn't until Jeannie heard the whining beside her that she found the will to move. Rolling over, she came nose to nose with Nugget. As if on cue, Nugget trotted over to Jeannie's closet and returned with one of her running shoes.

"That's a good boy, Nugget, but not today." She took the shoe and stroked the soft fur on top of his head.

Jeannie sensed the question lingering in his big brown eyes. "Don't worry. None of this has anything to do with you."

"I see Nugget isn't having any success getting you up either," her mother observed from the doorway. "I'm going to the grocery store, do you want to come?"

Jeannie shook her head.

Mrs. Fedorchak walked to the side of the bed and smiled softly at her daughter. "Try not to worry. The truth will set things right in time."

She looked up at her mother and frowned. "I want to believe that, but the waiting is torture. How long will it take before I know if Jason will forgive me?"

Her mother's expression was sympathetic. "I can't answer that, but if we could see what was in our future, we might miss out on the gifts the present has in store for us."

The honesty in her mother's words was sobering enough to cut through Jeannie's misery. "I just wanted a little peek."

Her mother laughed. "You know you prefer surprises."

Jeannie let out a sigh of resignation. "Then I might as well go on a run after all. I have a feeling staying in bed isn't going to make me feel any better."

"Be careful not to overdo it. The state meet is only a week away." Jeannie's mother leaned over to kiss her on the forehead before leaving the room.

For a second, Jeannie thought about inviting Emma, but she would be expecting to hear about her date with Jason, the one that never happened. That was something Jeannie wasn't ready to explain. "What about you, Nugget do you want to go on a run with me?"

Nugget, who had curled up in a spot on the floor, lifted his head and began thumping his tail. Jeannie pushed herself out of bed and went through the motions of getting dressed, even grabbing a sweatshirt to wear in case she got cold. She was trying to care about the upcoming meet, but it was difficult. Her heart felt so empty.

With Nugget's leash in hand she stepped outside and looked in both directions. She could either run her usual route down Dickson Street or take the other route by the high school that Emma had shown her. Nugget's excitement made the decision for her, as first Nugget then Jeannie began heading west toward the high school.

Jeannie was thankful for Nugget's gentle persistence on the end of the leash that kept them on a quick, even pace. It wasn't until they reached the street Mr. Trotter lived on that she hesitated. She turned the corner anyway with the hope they wouldn't see him.

The picture Jeannie encountered was serene and still. Only the tips of a few tree branches moved in answer to the occasional breeze. She glanced at each of the houses, having forgotten how similar they all looked in style and shape. Other than remembering Mr. Trotter's would be on her right, Jeannie couldn't make a positive identification.

They were halfway down the block when Nugget came to a dead stop. At first he just stood still, while Jeannie made futile attempts to encourage him on with the leash. Nugget's final response was to sit down, sending Jeannie the message that no amount of pulling was going to get him to budge.

"What's wrong, Nugget? I know it's been awhile since we've been on a run together, but you shouldn't be tired this soon." Jeannie looked around attempting to assess the problem.

Nugget seemed to listen to Jeannie while she spoke, but then turned his nose away as if he was taking orders from a different master.

Jeannie knew when she was defeated. She couldn't carry a fifty pound dog the rest of the way home. "All right, you win. We'll take a short rest, but you know this isn't good for my training."

If Nugget was remorseful, he didn't show it. He didn't even acknowledge Jeannie as she sat down on the curb beside him. Jeannie followed the line of Nugget's stare trying to determine what it was that had so completely captured her dog's attention. There was nothing.

Yet in the quiet of her mimicking gaze, Jeannie heard what she hadn't been able to see. The sound passed through Jeannie's ears straight to her heart. While faint, the melody was indisputable. It was Bach. Ever since she heard it on Dickson Street and again on her father's old cassettes, it had been infused in every part of her being.

The fortress of strength that usually came with running crumbled away with each measure of music. Jeannie was too beaten, emotionally and physically, to fight the tears that took over. She had never felt so alone nor missed her father so much. The painful reality that she would never have his comfort through such miserable heartache was too much.

With her head pressed against her knees, Jeannie hadn't noticed when the music stopped, only that it was no longer playing. That's when she heard footsteps accompanied by Nugget's obligatory bark. Jeannie's head jerked up as she wiped her hands across her face.

"Miss Fedorchak?"

Jeannie looked up to see a puzzled Mr. Trotter, embarrassment registering through her mind.

"I thought I recognized you sitting out here. Is everything all right?"

Jeannie allowed herself a moment to collect her composure before answering. "Yes, I was just out for a run when Nugget decided he needed a rest."

Nugget had already judged Mr. Trotter as a person he could get attention from, and Jeannie watched them greet each other with mutual affection.

"Do you mind if I join you two for a minute?" Mr. Trotter asked.

Jeannie shook her head, hoping the tear lines were invisible, though their dried remnants could still be felt on her cheeks.

Mr. Trotter sat down on the curb and continued to pet Nugget. "I had a dog named Maggie, but I lost her a few months ago. I suppose that's partly why I decided it was time for a new adventure and moved here. So far, I haven't had the heart to get a new dog."

Jeannie continued to watch their friendly exchange. "I'm sorry. I'd be happy to share Nugget with you."

Mr. Trotter turned to her and smiled. "Thank you."

"Jason told me how you happened to come to Perry," Jeannie said, pausing with a breath, "You know it's pretty hard to believe such a special Russian musician once lived right here and that he was your great uncle. Your name sure doesn't sound Russian."

Mr. Trotter chuckled. "My great uncle's name was Leopold Radgowsky and my mother was his niece. She was a Radgowsky, too, until she married a Frenchman and her last name became Trotter. But you're right, that a Russian band director escaped a revolution and ended up here is quite remarkable. It's often the truest stories that are. Now you can understand my inspiration behind the genealogy project. I think everyone should know their family's stories. It not only teaches us about history but about ourselves."

"So music runs in your family?" she asked, though she already knew the answer.

Mr. Trotter's eyebrows were raised. "I guess you could say it does. I play the cello."

The confirmation made the hair on Jeannie's arms stand up. If he only knew how she had been affected by his music. "I've heard you play."

"Very badly then I'm afraid. I haven't had much time to practice lately," he apologized.

"No, it was beautiful, and I happen to know Nugget agrees," Jeannie said while rubbing the fur down his back. "But I'm a little confused. The first time I heard a cello playing, I was on Dickson Street."

Mr. Trotter leaned his head back. "Ah, I was renting a room from Mrs. Latimer until this house was ready for me to move into."

"Mrs. Latimer, the librarian?"

"Yes. She's a very kind woman, and talented, too."

Jeannie realized they were talking more like friends than they were teacher and student, but there was an ease in his manner that made it seem like it was supposed to be that way. It was the same way her conversations with Jason had made her feel.

"I saw Mr. Butler earlier this morning. That's two of my students in one day," Mr. Trotter turned to her and said.

Jeannie's body froze in place. It was as if he had read her mind.

Mr. Trotter waited until Jeannie looked at him before he continued. "I noticed the same troubled look in his eyes that I see in yours. I hope it's nothing serious."

Jeannie was caught in his web of his concern, and there was no way out. The need to confide in someone overwhelmed her. "Mr. Trotter, I made a horrible mistake last night, and now Jason has the wrong idea about me and Brent Phillips."

Understanding spread across his face. "Am I correct that you don't have feelings for Mr. Phillips?"

"Not any good ones."

"But you do for Jason, don't you?"

Jeannie's shoulders dropped in surrender and she nodded her answer.

"I thought as much." Mr. Trotter smiled then added, "I don't pretend to be an expert in matters of the heart, but try not to worry. I do know that true love forgives."

Jeannie felt herself blush at his implication but did her best to return a smile. "I hope so."

They both stood up and Mr. Trotter gave Nugget one last pat. "I'm glad I got to meet you, Nugget."

"Maybe we can visit again. See you on Monday." Jeannie led off with the confidence of Mr. Trotter's words wrapped around her. *True love forgives...*

Jeannie could only hope he was right.

Chapter Twenty-six

The week that followed seemed to lengthen its hours just to torment Jeannie. She had gone to bed early every night hoping the closing of her eyes would provide an escape from her heartbreak, but it didn't. Images of Jason hid behind her eyelids sending her emotions on a runaway train she could neither steer nor stop.

She and Jason had been avoiding each other as if they were complete strangers, as if they had never met. Sometimes Jeannie wished they hadn't, except that she wasn't willing to discard the memories of the few good times they had already shared together.

Emma was sympathetic when Jeannie finally told her the whole story, but now she seemed to be making a point of getting to practice early just so she could talk to Jason. Seeing the two of them next to each other was difficult. While Jeannie realized he had the right to date whomever he wanted, the thought that it could be her best friend was almost unbearable. Emma would never care about him like she did, not while Brent was around.

The big event Jeannie had been training so hard for all season would be over in less than twenty-four hours. The fact that it was her last chance at a state title began to sink in as she tried to remember everything she had learned from Mr. Trotter. If only her heart were whole again, it might be easier.

Emma ran up to Jeannie as she was closing her locker after school. "Are we still on for tonight?"

Jeannie shrugged her shoulders. "Sure, I guess so."

"A little more enthusiasm might be good if we hope to have any chance of placing at state." Emma held a steady gaze on Jeannie. "Come on, I'm bringing over a special pasta dish I've renamed just for this event, *Pasta ala Emma*."

"You mean *Spaghetti ala Pizza Palace*." Jeannie broke a smile for the first time in days and was surprised at how much better it made her feel.

Emma returned the smile. "That's more like it. I'll see you at your house around 7:00."

Jeannie drove home with Emma's words repeating inside her head. She did need to snap out of it, especially since taking first and second at state had been her idea. She had never backed down from a challenge before and she wasn't about to start now.

She knew going for a run was out of the question, but Jeannie needed something to get her mind off the meet and off of Jason. As she approached the library, a sudden thought made her foot hit the brakes in time to slow down and turn into the parking lot. Once inside, Jeannie headed straight toward Mrs. Latimer's desk behind the circulation counter.

The empty chair filled Jeannie with disappointment. She looked around, deciding to wait and see if Mrs. Latimer had only stepped away and was coming back.

"Can I help you with something, hon?"

Jeannie's head swung around to see the assistant librarian looking at her. She knew right away who it was, even though she had never spoken with her before. For working in a quiet place, Darlene wore clothes that spoke loud and clear. Today's ensemble was a pair of purple slacks topped with a ruffled, fuchsia colored blouse. "I was hoping to talk to Mrs. Latimer."

"She had to leave early today. Is there anything I can help you with?"

Jeannie hesitated. Darlene was several years younger than Mrs. Latimer and probably wouldn't have any idea who Leopold Radgowsky was. "Someone told me that a Russian musician once lived here, and I was just wondering if the library had any information about him, that's all," she dismissed her inquiry with a wave of her hand.

"Thank you, anyway," Jeannie added as she turned to leave, thinking she must have sounded ridiculous.

"You mean the Professor?"

The question made Jeannie stop and swivel back around, "The Professor?"

Darlene appeared to withdraw a bit. "I really don't know very much, but I do know that's what everyone called him." Her voice then lowered to a whisper. "I think it was to keep his real identity a secret, you know being from Russia and all."

Jeannie chuckled in a return whisper. "Or maybe it was just easier to pronounce than his real name."

Seeming to ignore any practical explanation, Darlene kept going, "He was supposed to have been quite handsome, too."

Jeannie absorbed the information, becoming more and more intrigued that anyone like that would have ended up in Perry of all places. "How did you know about him?"

"I probably never would have if a gentleman hadn't come in over the summer asking Mrs. Latimer a whole lot of questions. As I recall, he paid her a number of visits. But don't go thinking I was eavesdropping. Mrs. Latimer came this close to breaking the library rule." Darlene pinched her fingers together to emphasize her point.

Jeannie was amused to hear Darlene's tattletale account of Mrs. Latimer's too loud talking, especially since she got the distinct impression that this woman loved gossip. And there wasn't an easier way to snoop than to simply overhear someone's conversation.

The gentleman she spoke of had to be Mr. Trotter, making Jeannie wonder what kinds of questions he was asking. "Do you remember anything else you heard?"

Darlene's mouth was already open, as if the words were propping her lips apart waiting to spill out. "All this gentleman and Mrs. Latimer talked about was music. They made this town sound famous all because of the Professor. Don't get me wrong, he may have been an actual celebrity, but nothing like Mack Johnson when he and his record-breaking pumpkin got on the news."

As much as Jeannie loved pumpkins for all sorts of reasons, she didn't think they came close to the enduring power of music. "It's too bad there's probably no one left in this town that ever got to meet him."

"Oh, but there is," Darlene's voice rang.

When Jeannie returned a blank stare, Darlene continued, "I thought that was why you were looking for

Mrs. Latimer. After all it was her mother the Professor rented a room from."

Jeannie's mind began to race. Could it be that the mother's house was the same one on Dickson Street that Mrs. Latimer lived in now? That would mean that Mr. Trotter may have stayed in the same room that his great uncle did years earlier. Jeannie could only imagine all the music the walls of that house had been an audience to.

"I'm sorry I don't have more to tell you. Mrs. Latimer will be here tomorrow if you want to come back."

Darlene's words drew Jeannie back to attention. "That's okay. You've helped me more than you know."

Jeannie left the library entranced by what Darlene had told her. Her thoughts traveled back in time as she tried to picture what Mr. Trotter's great uncle may have looked like. If he was as handsome as he was rumored to be, she was surprised he managed to escape the clutches of women inevitably vying for his attention.

Maybe it was because his heart had already been spoken for and left in the care of another woman back in Russia, someone he may have known he would never see again. Jeannie was overcome with the sadness she presumed he must have felt when he had to leave her.

A honk from the car behind jolted her from her make-believe mourning long enough to realize how slow she was driving and to speed up. Her thoughts then returned to its one act play. She envisioned the faces of two people being forced apart, possibly forever, neither one able to release their grip on the other. But what if they never even got to say good-bye?

Jeannie's heart beat in aching rhythm for their unfulfilled love, or if she was being honest, for her and Jason. Their separation had been all her fault. At least Leopold had a revolution to blame.

Chapter Twenty-seven

Jeannie arrived home, noticing right away there was a package on the front porch. From what she could tell it was a small box, just large enough not to fit inside the mailbox. She couldn't remember her mother mentioning she had ordered anything.

She parked her car then hurried up the porch steps, wanting to find out where it was from. When Jeannie reached down to pick it up, large black letters appeared to lift themselves off the brown paper to meet her eyes. The name, Fedorchak, was written in a handwriting that resembled Aunt Maria's. A look at the return address confirmed she was right, though Aunt Maria had never sent them a package before, not even at Christmas.

The box was light enough to tuck under her arm while she fumbled through her keys to find the one to the front door. Nugget started barking from inside. "It's all right, Nugget," Jeannie called as she pushed open the door. "Sorry I took so long."

She gave Nugget a reassuring stroke then took the box in both hands and gave it a slight shake. Whatever was inside didn't sound breakable, though there was only one way to be sure.

For a slight moment Jeannie wondered if she should wait for her mother to get home. Then she gazed at the name again. The package must be meant for both of them or it would have had more than just their last name. Jeannie took hold of the paper and ripped until all that was left in her hands was an old cardboard box. Her breathing was heavy with anticipation as she lifted up each flap.

Jeannie stared at the contents, blinking her eyes a couple of times to maintain their focus. A stack of what looked to be old letters were bundled and tied together with a frayed piece of pink satin ribbon. She reached in and lifted them out with her eyes glued to the writing on the top envelope. It was addressed to Maria Winston. Jeannie's mind raced back to the magazine she had found in the living room at Aunt Maria's house. That was the name printed on its label.

After carefully separating the letter from the rest of the bundle, Jeannie opened the envelope and pulled out the papers. In a single glance, it was obvious there was nothing she would be able to read. The words weren't in English. Her eyes roughly scanned through the lines until she reached the end of the letter. It was there that Jeannie's heart lurched. She would know Grandma Sophia's signature anywhere. Her fingers grazed the ink, as she inspected the words again more closely, trying to figure out what language it was.

Jeannie untied the ribbon from around the rest of the envelopes, estimating there to be around a dozen letters. The first few were similar, but then both the handwriting and the name changed. These were instead written by Aunt Maria to Grandma Sophia. Jeannie wasted no time in pulling out those letters, hoping there would be at least one that she could read. There wasn't.

The resulting pile of paper and envelopes produced a sigh of disappointment. Frustrated, Jeannie started to put them back in the box until a small piece of paper left inside stopped her. She took it out, glad to see at least a few words written in English.

It's time you know. Maria

"It's time I know what?" Jeannie looked at the pile of opened letters. "And how am I ever supposed to find out?"

Nugget answered her question with a sigh of his own, raising his head as if he were in complete agreement with her.

"I don't suppose you know how to speak other languages," she asked him. The earnestness in his cocked head and raised eyebrows made her laugh. "I didn't think so."

"Jeannie?" Her mother walked into the entryway and glanced around. "Oh, I thought I heard you talking to someone."

Jeannie was surprised she hadn't heard her mother come home. The side door into the kitchen almost always squeaked. "It was only me having a conversation with Nugget about the package that was delivered today." Jeannie picked up the pile of letters and held them out in front of her. "These are what were inside."

Mrs. Fedorchak's eyes darted from the papers in Jeannie's hands to her face. "Those look like old letters. Who sent them?"

"Aunt Maria." Jeannie paused to let her answer sink in. "Why don't I put them on the dining room table so you can look at them." Jeannie led the way to the table and laid them down.

Jeannie's mother was careful as she picked up each envelope and its corresponding letter, turning over each page as if she were actually reading it. "I can hardly believe it. These are letters written between Maria and your grandmother."

"Any chance you know what they say?" Jeannie's voice was cautiously optimistic.

"Not in the least." Her mother shook her head. "I'm stunned they still exist. I wonder what kept Maria from destroying them like she did almost everything else from their past?"

"She did say that it was time we knew." Jeannie handed her mother the note that had been clutched in her fingers. "Whatever that's supposed to mean?"

Mrs. Fedorchak stared at the paper then set it on the table beside the letters. Her frustration duplicated Jeannie's. "I suppose we should be grateful she sent them, but what possible good are they to us."

"I guess I can include one in my genealogy project. At least no one else will be able to read it either, just in case it contains a great family secret."

"You don't really think we have one, do you?" her mother asked.

"Probably not, but it does make our lives sound more intriguing, don't you think?" Jeannie grinned.

Her mother shook her head. "I could do with less intrigue, thank you."

"Speaking of intriguing, I stopped by the library on my way home and found out a few more things about our Russian musician who used to live here."

"Since when did he become *our* Russian musician?"

"You never know. We might be related." Jeannie giggled while placing her hand on top of the letters. "Maybe these are written in Russian. At least he would have been able to read them."

Jeannie's mother took a glimpse at the clock. "Well, before your imagination has us kin to the tsar, I should start dinner. That is unless you have other plans."

"You don't need to fix me anything. Emma offered to bring pasta over later tonight. She thinks it will give us the extra boost of energy we need for the meet tomorrow." Jeannie's expression turned pensive before she added, "Our last one ever."

Jeannie's mother took hold of her daughter's shoulders and looked her straight in the eye. "I'm very proud of you no matter what the outcome is. You've worked hard these past few years, and you have the cross-country record to prove it."

Jeannie nodded. "Don't worry. I'll be okay whatever happens. I think I'll go upstairs for awhile and take these letters with me. Who knows, maybe if I stare at them long enough the blood of my ancestors running through my veins will give me the special power to read them."

Once she was in her bedroom, Jeannie picked up a pencil and pad of paper from her desk and began copying one of the pages written by her grandmother. Her fingers took slow and deliberate care, forming each of the letters as close to identical as she could get them, some of them looking the same as in English. Jeannie wanted to believe the impossible, that some sort of magical exchange was taking place between the pencil and her brain. That if she kept to the task long enough, she would soon be able to translate what the words meant.

Some words were repeated often enough that she tried to guess, but in the end they were still just as foreign. Jeannie plopped the pad and pencil down on her desk in surrender, though she hadn't really expected any miracles. She laid her head down and had closed her eyes to rest when the doorbell rang. A quick check of her clock registered disbelief. It was 7:00 already. A grumble from her stomach testified how much time had passed.

Jeannie left her room knowing that her mother would have already answered the door and let Emma inside by now. Her mouth was open and ready to speak when she reached the bottom of the stairs, but nothing came out. The picture in front of her was so similar to the dreams her heart had tried to create. There, only a few feet away from her, stood Jason Butler. Surely, this wasn't some cruel trick of her mind.

"Are you going to speak, Jeannie?" her mother asked.

Jeannie had failed to pay attention to the fact that her mother was standing right next to him. "Um…..hi."

Mrs. Fedorchak gave a wink only Jeannie was able to see. "If you two will excuse me, I have some work to do in the kitchen. It's nice to see you again, Jason."

"Thank you, Mrs. Fedorchak." Jason watched her leave then turned toward Jeannie. "I hope it's all right I'm here."

The sound of his voice lifted Jeannie's heart. "Yes…of course. I'm just…"

"Surprised?"

"After what happened last weekend, I didn't expect you to ever speak to me again. I wouldn't blame you either."

Jason motioned toward the sofa. "Do you mind if we sit down?"

Jeannie walked over and sat on one end of the sofa while Jason sat in the middle toward the edge. He rested his arms on his legs with his hands clasped together.

"I don't blame you for anything, Jeannie. I owe you an apology for not giving you a chance to explain. Thankfully, someone set me straight." What started as half a grin turned into a full smile as he turned to face Jeannie, "Everyone should be lucky to have a friend like Emma. If I hadn't seen her at practice, I'm sure she would have figured out another way to let me know what happened."

Jeannie was relieved to know the real reason Emma was getting to practices early. Jason was right. She was a great friend. "What did she tell you?"

Jason's smile disappeared as he answered. "I don't know the details. Only that you were trying to help your mother even if it meant sacrificing an evening to be with Brent Phillips. Emma made it clear how much you disliked him. You swallowed your pride much better than I did."

What Jeannie had to swallow now was the repugnant feeling the mention of Brent's name gave her. But one look at Jason, knowing he forgave her, made it dissipate.

"When I saw you dressed up that night and then Brent came…I have to admit I was more than a little jealous. I'm sorry." Jason's thumbs tapped against each other as he finished.

Jeannie waited for him to look at her again. "I'm sorry, too. I should have known better than to play one of Brent's games."

"Dinner's on the table you two," her mother called from the dining room.

Her mother's timing was perfect, but Jeannie was suddenly confused. "I'm supposed to be eating with Emma. She said she was going to bring over…"

"Pasta a la Emma?" Jason completed the sentence for her, his sheepish grin telling her this was all part of a plan.

Her mother peeked around the corner. "It's more like Chicken Tetrazzini, Fedorchak style."

In the brief moment Jeannie's eyes met her mother's, she knew her mother had been in on it, too.

Jason stood up before helping Jeannie stand beside him. "Shall we?"

If the state meet had been occurring at that very moment, Jeannie's heart would have flown her over the finish line. But right now, holding Jason's hand, nothing else in the world mattered.

Chapter Twenty-eight

Jeannie didn't remember falling asleep, but she woke up early the next morning feeling rested and ready to run. After a light breakfast and an hour drive, she and Emma were standing in the warm-up area waiting for the race to begin. Jeannie wished Jason had qualified for the state meet, too. He was a good runner, and she had no doubt with a little more experience he would have been suited up with them.

Jeannie's eyes found where Jason and her mother were standing, prompting another smile to spread across her face, one of many she had been unable to contain since the night before.

"I've never seen anyone smile so much this early in the morning. It's rather sickening you know." Emma lifted her eyes in mock disgust.

Jeannie's smile only grew. "It's your fault for being such a good friend and for helping to fix things between Jason and me."

Emma finished a stretch to each side then paused to smile back. "Don't think I'm going to let you forget it either."

Jeannie watched as Emma's focus suddenly lowered and she stepped closer toward her. Without any warning she flicked her hand across Jeannie's shoulder.

"What was that for?" Jeannie looked off to the side trying to figure out what she had missed.

Emma laughed. "Don't worry. It was just a harmless ladybug."

As soon as Jeannie heard the word ladybug she was down on her hands and knees in the grass. "Did you see where she went?"

"Not really." Emma's answer was joined by another stretch.

Jeannie raised her head to make a desperate plea. "I need you to help me find her... please."

Emma abandoned the lunged position she was in and knelt down on the ground beside her. "If this isn't crazy, I don't know what is. Why are we looking for an insect on one of the biggest days of our lives?"

"I promise I'll explain after we find her. We have to hurry," Jeannie's tone was urgent.

Both pairs of hands began sifting through the blades of grass in the area the ladybug should have landed. Within minutes Emma was lifting her finger in slow motion. "Here she is, though I feel a bit ridiculous calling something with six legs a *she*."

Jeannie let the ladybug crawl into the palm of one hand before covering it with the other and slowly stood back up. "What else would you call a lady?"

Emma was brushing the dirt and grass off her knees when she stopped and took a hard look at Jeannie. "You're starting to worry me. Are you all right?"

Jeannie laughed at her best friend's voice of concern. "I've never been better. Ladybugs are supposed to bring good luck you know."

"I hope you're right," Emma laughed with her.

Neither of the girls noticed Mr. Trotter walking up from behind. "It's almost time to line up. Are you girls ready?"

Jeannie glanced from her clasped hands, to Emma, to Mr. Trotter. "We're ready."

"I want you to remember that you both have as good a chance to win as any other runner on this field. Stay focused and don't forget to keep your eye on..."

Jeannie held her breath while Mr. Trotter continued to speak, hoping he wouldn't put his fist out and expect them to do the team's special handshake. She didn't want him to know she was holding a ladybug, even though he had been the one to tell her about their bringing good luck. Telling him before the race might jinx it, never mind that Emma already knew.

She was relieved when he said, "See you at the finish line," and she watched him turn around and leave.

Once Mr. Trotter was a distance away, she placed the ladybug inside the small zippered pocket on the front of her shorts. "Sophia is about to go on the ride of her life."

"What! You named it?" Emma quickly put her hands up. "Sorry, I mean her."

Jeannie nodded. "After one of the finest ladies I've known."

Emma shook her head. "You are going to set her free after this is over, right?"

"Of course," Jeannie answered with a grin before walking over to join the line-up. Emma got into place several girls down from her.

The temperature was somewhat chilly, yet mild for the first Saturday of November. Jeannie thought it was the perfect weather to run in, considering what the alternative could have been. One never knew how Mother Nature would act this time of year. It was a daily ritual of forecast roulette and could just as easily have been anything from freezing to eighty degrees.

Jeannie patted the pocket that contained her tiny cargo of luck and nodded at Emma just before the gun sounded. The new strategy they had been using at the other meets was about to be given its ultimate test.

It was difficult not to panic amidst the explosion of speeding legs, but this was the part Jeannie did well. Even now, competing against the best, she was able to press toward the front of the pack while controlling the adrenalin that encouraged her to run faster. Jeannie spotted Emma a short distance in front of her, right where she was supposed to be. In a few moments Jeannie would increase her pace just enough to take the lead for a while. They would then continue to take turns, never losing sight of each other all the way to the final stretch.

It was Jeannie's turn in the lead when she saw a green uniform out of the corner of her eye and the face that had haunted her all season. *Not this time you don't*. She used the thought to fight back memories from the opening meet when this girl had beaten her. Jeannie was careful to release only the amount of energy needed to maintain an advantage and not get so far ahead that Emma couldn't catch up.

The number of runners ahead of her had thinned out, but seeing the curve in the course she knew they were getting close to the last half mile. She expected Emma to take the lead one last time before they both ran with all their might.

The sound of labored breathing alerted Jeannie first, and then the half-spouted words, "I can't…"

"Stay with me, Emma."

"…trying..."

Within a few more yards Jeannie knew she was on her own and that placing in this race was now up to her. She could see the runners in front of her and just beyond them, the crowd that was cheering with what sounded like one giant voice. Jason and her mother were in the crowd somewhere, but it would have been impossible to locate them.

She had to keep going. She couldn't give up now, though the intense burning she felt throughout her body would have made it easy. Then Jeannie heard the voice meant just for her. "Come on, Fedorchak. Keep fighting."

It was Mr. Trotter. The words spurred Jeannie forward, reminding her of what he drilled into the team at every practice, "When you think you've given all you can, give more." Yet it was also a sense of pride in hearing her last name that rallied her spirit of determination.

Jeannie drove herself past the first girl in front of her and continued pressing toward the next. She seemed to be gaining speed, feeding off the energy from each opponent she passed until there was only one girl left ahead of her. Her hunger to win had never been this strong.

The noise from the crowd grew more deafening the closer they got to the end. Jeannie lengthened her stride and tried to ignore the nagging concern that there might not be enough ground left to beat her. That's when she saw Jason, his smile beaming like a lighthouse to guide her across this stormy sea of grass.

...give more... Fedorchak... The words echoed faster and faster in Jeannie's mind, churning into an engine that generated a power she didn't know she possessed. With one final effort she stretched her legs across the finish line.

The next few moments were a blur of excitement as Jeannie was swooped up in her mother's arms followed by hugs from Mr. Trotter and Jason. She must have won, but it all seemed too surreal, and where was Emma?

A hand touched her shoulder from behind, causing Jeannie to turn around and see the familiar pair of blue eyes surrounded by a red splotched face.

"Congratulations," Emma managed to say before they collapsed against each other. "I'm so proud of you."

Jeannie pushed herself back to get a better look at Emma, "I just wish..."

As if Emma knew what Jeannie was going to say she quickly interrupted, "I know we were hoping to take first and second place, but considering I've never run in the state meet before, I'll take tenth place any day."

"Tenth! That's fantastic, Emma. I was so afraid you couldn't hold on anymore."

"Are you kidding? When I saw where you were headed, I wasn't about to quit trying."

Jeannie put out her fist for Emma to complete the team handshake, ending with a high five. The action produced a flushed reminder of what was still in her pocket. That a ladybug's life might have been sacrificed for her cause filled Jeannie's heart with pangs of unease.

She unzipped what she hoped hadn't become a tomb and stuck one finger inside to carefully comb the edges. When it found the miniature bump, it stopped. To Jeannie's relief, she soon felt the gentle tickle of legs crawling up her finger. By the time she pulled it out, everyone was watching her. She leaned down and placed it back in the grass, taking a moment for her thoughts. *Good-bye, Sophia. Thank you.*

"How odd that a ladybug found its way into your pocket," Jeannie's mother remarked.

Jeannie shared a knowing look with Mr. Trotter and Emma. "I guess she just felt like racing today."

Chapter Twenty-nine

It was Monday, two days after the state meet, and Jeannie still felt the need to pinch herself to make sure she wasn't being fooled by one very long and realistic dream. The race and the celebration afterwards at the Pizza Palace had been the happiest day of her life. There were somber moments, however, when Jeannie wanted to believe her father was looking down on her, sharing in her victory as well.

Words of congratulations followed her into world history where Mr. Trotter had written them across the blackboard. "It's not every day we have a first place state champion in our class," he said, motioning a hand toward Jeannie, "so in honor of Miss Fedorchak, I decided to postpone our lesson for today."

Whistles of approval were punctuated with, "Way to go, Jeannie."

While Jeannie appreciated the show of support, she sensed something different about the noise. Something was missing. She turned around just enough to catch a glimpse of the class and realize what it was. Brent was at his desk with his mouth closed. For some reason, he was keeping his usual attention-seeking comments to himself. Jeannie knew she should be thankful, but the shift from his familiar behavior was as unsettling as it was curious.

Mr. Trotter's voice was quick to intercede. "There is an assignment, however, even if the only requirement is to listen. You might see some questions on the next test just to see if you did. The first order of business, however, is your genealogy project. How many of you have it completed?"

A small number of hands rose.

"How many are close to having it completed?"

A few more hands went up, including Jason's this time. Jeannie's remained down, as well as Brent's. She figured his only excuse was laziness.

"There's only a few more weeks left until they're due, so you'll want to be finishing them up. Moving on, I thought I'd read the poem by my great uncle again. Then I'll explain how he ended up living right here in Perry."

Heads turned from side to side in question. Jeannie knew some of the story, but she looked forward to hearing more of it from Mr. Trotter. All eyes were focused on him as he read. This time Jeannie had a better understanding of the words and what they meant.

Mr. Trotter looked up when he finished. "We haven't studied the Russian revolution yet, but to put it simply, there was an uprising in 1917 that overthrew Tsar Nicholas II and ended centuries of Imperial rule in Russia. My great uncle, whose name was Leopold Radgowsky, was the conductor of the Tsar's Imperial Band at that time. He was also a man of royal heritage, which made him a target of the revolutionaries. His only choice was to escape or be executed."

A long pause stretched the silence in the room. It was as if Mr. Trotter's words were on feathers, floating down slowly into the minds of everyone in the class, waiting for him to continue.

"He was fortunate to make it to Paris where he met up with some other Russian musicians and formed a band. It so happened they were playing in London at the same time the 101 Ranch Wild West Show was touring Europe, and they were hired to be part of the show. In case you don't know, the 101 Ranch was a famous ranch that used to be located a short distance northeast of here."

Mr. Trotter's last few words made Jeannie think of her Uncle John who also lived northeast of Perry. It made her wonder if she and her mother had driven by where this ranch used to be and not even known it.

"After the tour, the band was brought back to the ranch, but financial problems arose and they weren't rehired. Some of the band went back to Europe, but with the continued threat on his life, Leopold chose to stay here. He spoke little English and had no money, only the friendship of another performer who helped him start his new life teaching music."

"A real live Russian hiding out in Perry?" a voice rang with skepticism.

Mr. Trotter smiled then nodded. "He became Perry's first full-time band director. He also started an orchestra program, though it didn't survive after he died.

"Who listens to that kind of music anyway?" The sneering remark came from Brent whose old self seemed to have returned.

Mr. Trotter's reaction appeared to be one of amusement. "You do, Mr. Phillips, unless you never watch television, or see any movies."

Many in the class chuckled, including Jeannie. She knew Mr. Trotter's words were layered with sarcasm, though his voice never gave it away.

Mr. Trotter continued, "I can provide you with some examples if you'd like."

Brent's smug dismissal of the offer gave Jeannie an opportunity to clarify something Mr. Trotter had said earlier. She raised her hand.

"Yes, Miss Fedorchak."

Jeannie couldn't keep from grinning as she asked, "If your great uncle was considered royalty, wouldn't that make you royalty, too?"

Mr. Trotter offered a grin in return. "What little royal blood there was only ran through my mother's veins, not my father's, though none of that matters anymore."

"Do you know how to speak Russian?" another classmate asked.

Mr. Trotter shook his head. "Not well. I can read it better."

It took a moment for the impact of Mr. Trotter's last words to explode into Jeannie's thoughts. *The letters!* Maybe he would have an idea what language the letters between her grandmother and Aunt Maria were written in. If by chance they were written in Russian, he might be able to translate them. They had to contain something important or Aunt Maria's note wouldn't make sense.

Her eyes began to swing like a pendulum between Mr. Trotter and the clock as if they themselves could speed the time up until the end of class. It was impossible to pay attention to anything else being said.

Once the bell rang, Jeannie walked back to where Mr. Trotter had returned to his desk.

"Mr. Trotter, may I ask you something?"

"Of course," he answered.

Jeannie suddenly felt apprehensive. "It's actually a favor I need."

Mr. Trotter gave her his full attention. "How can I help you?"

"We received some old letters between my grandmother and my aunt, but they aren't in English. Today, you said you could read Russian so I wondered if you would take a look at them. Maybe you'll know what language they're written in, even if you can't read them."

All her words ran together, making Mr. Trotter smile. "So that's why you were fidgeting at your desk for most of the class."

Jeannie felt embarrassment creep up her neck and spill onto her face. She should have known he would notice.

"I would be happy to give them a look," he completed his answer.

Jeannie thought fast. "I could hurry home after school and bring them up to you. That is if you don't mind waiting a few extra minutes."

"I always stay for a while, so that would be fine."

Jeannie bounced out of the room. She could hardly wait until school was out.

Chapter Thirty

Jeannie glanced at her speedometer and eased her foot off the accelerator. She was anxious to get back to the school, though, preferably, without getting a speeding ticket.

The bundle of letters sat in the seat beside her. Having been kept silent for years, Jeannie sensed a purpose in their presence. There had to be a reason her grandmother mentioned them, a reason greater than just the ordinary exchange of correspondence between two sisters. Jeannie scoffed at the latter thought. From what she observed, the relationship between Maria and Sophia had never been anything close to ordinary.

With most of the cars gone, Jeannie was able to pull into a parking space close to the front door. She grabbed the letters and entered the school, turning left toward the world history classroom. A few other teachers were still there, but otherwise the hallways were empty, becoming the perfect vessel to amplify every sound. Jeannie's head snapped around once before she realized the footsteps and breathing were hers alone.

When she reached the doorway, she saw Mr. Trotter at his desk focused on a piece of paper he held in his hands.

Jeannie hesitated at first not wanting to disturb him, but she knew he was expecting her to return. She knocked lightly against the wood frame.

Mr. Trotter's eyes went from Jeannie to the clock and back again before he smiled. "That was an awfully quick trip."

Jeannie hid a twinge of guilt. "I didn't want to keep you waiting for me. If you're doing something important, I can bring the letters back another time."

"You mean this?" He lifted up the paper. "No, I was only hoping to get your opinion."

Jeannie walked over and sat down in the extra chair he had beside his desk.

Mr. Trotter turned the paper around so she could see what it was he had been so engrossed in. "What do you think? Is there a family resemblance?"

A copy of an old photograph was the last thing Jeannie expected to be giving an opinion on. It pictured a stern looking man bearing a thick moustache and dressed in what appeared to be a military uniform. "That's a picture of your great uncle?"

Mr. Trotter nodded.

Jeannie's eyes pivoted back and forth between the picture and Mr. Trotter. "Not really, but then again it is hard to tell with the moustache and the uniform, neither of which I'd recommend."

Mr. Trotter laughed while Jeannie looked at the great uncle's face more closely. Underneath the harsh line of the moustache she detected the soft placement of his mouth, and in his dark eyes, an intense but compassionate wisdom.

He held himself straight and proud, but there was something much more complex about him.

"I wonder what he was thinking about when that picture was taken," Jeannie finally said.

Mr. Trotter's head tilted as he looked at his great uncle again. "I've wondered that, too. He lost a family, a home and a country. I'm sure those memories were never far away."

They stared at the picture a moment more as if they were both trying to imagine themselves in his place. Then Mr. Trotter laid it aside. "Now, let me see these letters you brought."

Jeannie handed the bundle to Mr. Trotter. "I've divided them into those from my aunt and those from my grandmother. I was surprised they were written in their native language as much as Maria seemed to want to forget her past. But I suppose they had to be or my grandmother wouldn't have been able to read them."

Mr. Trotter picked up the letter off the top and held it thoughtfully between his fingers. "Many immigrants felt the way your aunt did. They were so eager to shed their old way of life that once they set foot on American soil, they threw away the clothes on their backs as soon as they could put new ones on. Trash cans and ditches were filled with the remnants of discarded lives."

It was difficult for Jeannie to understand how putting on new clothes would be all it took to become a new person. How could you ever forget who you were and where you came from? Her thoughts returned to the letters as she watched Mr. Trotter open one from her grandmother and begin looking at it.

Jeannie kept her eyes on Mr. Trotter's face, hoping to glean something from his expressions. His eyebrows, however, remained firmly squeezed together, revealing nothing to her. It was so quiet Jeannie could hear her heart competing against the constant tick of the clock.

After looking at only the front side of the paper, Mr. Trotter set it down and looked at Jeannie, relaxing his eyebrows a little as he spoke, "What country is it your grandmother and aunt came from?"

"Austria, though I've since learned it was really Austria-Hungary at that time," Jeannie answered.

Mr. Trotter's head nodded slowly in response.

"Is there something wrong?" Jeannie felt a sudden anxiety.

"No, not at all," Mr. Trotter waved his hand to dismiss her concern. "The Austro-Hungarian Empire consisted of several different ethnic groups, a few using the same Cyrillic alphabet that the Russian language does. If these aren't in Russian, they're very close. I should be able to translate most of it for you."

Jeannie almost bounced out of the chair. "Thank you, Mr. Trotter."

He laughed at her excitement. "Don't thank me just yet. I'm a little rusty so it may take a while."

Jeannie was getting ready to ask another question when she was interrupted by loud, clunking footsteps coming down the hallway. There was only one thing that made that sound… cowboy boots.

Both heads shot up when they seemed to stop right outside Mr. Trotter's door. They glanced at each other as if the other's face might hold the clue as to who the footsteps belonged to. Without an answer, Mr. Trotter stood up from his chair just as the steps turned away, diminishing in sound until they could no longer hear them.

"I guess whoever it was changed their mind." Mr. Trotter shrugged his shoulders and sat back down, "Now where were we?"

Jeannie tried to draw her attention back to the letters and picture on his desk, but phantom echoes of footsteps kept intruding each thought. "How about taking the letters home with you? That way you can translate them whenever you have time."

Mr. Trotter smiled. "Are you sure you trust me with them?"

"It looks like I'll have to if I want to find out what they say," she teased him back.

Returning a more serious gaze, Mr. Trotter looked at Jeannie. "I know how valuable these letters are to you. I promise I will handle them with the utmost care."

"I know you will. Thanks again, Mr. Trotter." Jeannie got up and left the room, feeling slightly unsettled. Someone else had just been in this same hallway, as close as Mr. Trotter's door, and for some unknown reason left.

All she knew for sure was the person wore cowboy boots. But then, so did at least a hundred other students at the school.

Chapter Thirty-one

A chill was present in the air, but receding rays from the late afternoon sun offered Jeannie a small amount of warmth once she was outside and heading back toward her car. She knew it wouldn't be long before the cold weather set in for good, and with one look at her car, was reminded she should wash it before then.

Her hand reached out to open the door when an arm swung against it to stop her. Jeannie jumped back, startled. Then her eyes locked onto Brent's. "What do you think you're doing?"

He didn't answer. His breathing was quick and shallow, and his entire being seemed to twitch with agitation.

"Was that you in the hallway outside Mr. Trotter's room?" Jeannie tried another question, keeping her voice steady, despite her growing level of discomfort.

"Maybe," Brent stepped closer toward Jeannie. "Maybe I went to see Mr. Trotter, but he was busy talking to someone, someone who turned out to be you."

"Is there something you want, because I'm not in the mood for any more of your games," Jeannie reached again for the handle.

This time Brent shoved his body in between her and the door, completely blocking her attempt.

Jeannie's discomfort gave way to anger. "Get out of my way, Brent."

Brent's eyes narrowed. "You knew about me, didn't you? That's why I've never been good enough for you."

"I have no idea what you're talking about, only that you'll do anything to get your way. So I guess you're right, you're not good enough for me. Now if you would please move, I need to get home," Jeannie's tone was firm.

Brent pressed forward, forcing Jeannie away from her car. "You know I was counting on that good night kiss after the rodeo banquet."

"You're kidding, right?" she mocked, continuing to back away. "That would never have happened."

Jeannie tried to halt his advances but lost her balance when he unexpectedly grabbed her arms. She turned her head and closed her eyes, causing her to miss seeing the arm that swept underneath Brent's shoulder and locked behind his neck. It wasn't until she felt the immediate release of his hold that her eyes flew open to a shocking sight. Mr. Trotter had Brent in a firm hold with one of his hands pinned behind his back.

"Let me go," Brent yelled through clenched teeth.

Mr. Trotter pushed Brent's head farther against his chest. "You're not going anywhere yet."

"Just try and keep me here." Brent struggled to wrench himself away, but his body might as well have been inside a Chinese finger trap. The harder he fought, the tighter Mr. Trotter's grasp became.

Jeannie was frozen in place, watching determination drip from the pores of Mr. Trotter's face. Judging from his lean frame she would never have guessed him to be capable of such strength.

Mr. Trotter's eyes found Jeannie's. "Are you all right?"

Jeannie nodded while swallowing to be able to speak again. "I'm fine."

"What's going on here," a man's gruff voice belted from a short distance away in the parking lot.

They turned to see Mr. Phillips fast approaching them.

Mr. Trotter didn't release his hold on Brent until his father had reached them. "Your son appeared to have dishonorable intentions toward Miss Fedorchak."

Brent flung his body away from his captor. "I'm not his son." Then casting a cold glare toward Mr. Phillips, he challenged, "Am I? When were you going to tell me I was adopted?"

All eyes were on Mr. Phillips whose face had lost its color. "It's why I came looking for you. We can discuss this at home, Brent."

"I don't have a home anymore." Brent then pointed to Mr. Trotter to continue, "Thanks to your stupid genealogy project. You should have stayed in the city where you belong."

The resulting silence was filled with the stomp of Brent's boot heels against the pavement. It wasn't until he drove off in his pickup that anyone spoke again. By then a flush of red had returned to Mr. Phillips face. "I could have you fired for this."

Mr. Trotter showed no evidence of feeling threatened, "I think you better concentrate on your son's behavior toward this young woman and figure out why you thought it was a good idea not to tell him about this apparent adoption."

"I already know why. It was to protect him," Mr. Phillips fired back.

"Yet, Miss Fedorchak was the one needing protection today," Mr. Trotter emphasized. "She could press charges against Brent, if she so chooses."

Jeannie took Mr. Trotter's lead and lifted her chin to face Mr. Phillips eye to eye. In spite of knowing how he treated the Butlers and interfered with her mother's promotion, the startling revelation of Brent's adoption made her almost pity him. For all his power, he may have lost his only child forever.

Mr. Phillips turned and walked away without saying another word.

It was a moment before Mr. Trotter looked at Jeannie again only this time his expression was full of apprehension. "Are you sure he didn't hurt you or do anything…"

Jeannie shook her head. "No, thanks to you and that hold you put him in. How did you do that?"

"It's a wrestling move I learned a long time ago. I sure never thought I'd be using it again, especially because of a genealogy assignment." Mr. Trotter still looked concerned.

"Mr. Trotter, it's not your fault Brent found out the truth. My mother has always said that a skeleton kept in the closet will start rattling its bones sooner or later."

Mr. Trotter's expression lightened slightly. "Your mother is right."

Jeannie was glad to see him a little more relaxed and glanced at her watch. "I guess I should be going now."

"Will your mother be home from work?"

"Not for a little while, but Nugget's there waiting for me."

A corner of Mr. Trotter's mouth lifted into half a grin. "Ah, then I'm sure I needn't worry. However, I'd feel much better if you would allow me to escort you there."

Jeannie drove out of the parking lot with Mr. Trotter behind her. Not knowing what Brent's angry state was capable of, she was glad he was following her home. Once she unlocked the door and went inside, she waved to Mr. Trotter, waiting in the street. Jeannie expected him to leave right away, but it wasn't until after she gave Nugget his usual amount of attention that she looked out the window and saw him drive off.

Other than her father, Jeannie couldn't imagine another man more perfect for her mother. He was smart and kind and strong. He was also her friend. But as much as she wanted her mother to find love again, Jeannie knew no amount of matchmaking could make it happen. If it was going to take a strike of lightening, she would just have to pray for a storm.

Chapter Thirty-two

Jeannie rubbed the places on her arms where Brent had grabbed her. At the time she hadn't felt frightened, but remembering the cold indifference she had seen in his eyes set off an unexpected shudder. She sat down on the sofa and tried to steer her thoughts away from what he might have done had Mr. Trotter not shown up. Knowing how close she came to feeling Brent's lips touch hers caused a knot of disgust to form in her stomach.

She still couldn't believe he was adopted. His features were so much like his father's that no one would suspect they weren't blood related. But then Emma looked a lot like her mother, and she was adopted, too. Maybe family traits were influenced by more than shared DNA. Maybe time was its own sculptor, blending together all of their unique characteristics.

Jeannie's contemplations came to an abrupt end as she heard the kitchen door burst open and a set of keys hit the table.

"Jeannie?"

"In here, Mom."

Jeannie's mother rushed into the living room towards the sofa, and within seconds her arms were wrapped around her daughter. After a long moment she pulled back.

Jeannie studied the different emotions assembled on her mother's face. Her eyes were filled with worry, yet her mouth was pressed into a firm line of anger she had never seen before. "How did you know?"

"Mr. Trotter came by my office before I left." Her expression softened only until she spoke again. "If Brent Phillips hurt you in any way…"

"I'm okay, Mom," Jeannie cut in, taking hold of her mother's hand for reassurance. "What did Mr. Trotter tell you?"

Her mother caught her breath before she answered. "He said that he met with you after school. Then as he left the building, he saw you by your car struggling to get away from Brent. Mr. Trotter said he was able to stop him, and then I don't remember what I heard after that. I was in such a hurry to get home."

Picturing Mr. Trotter's hold on Brent made Jeannie let out a soft snicker. "Mr. Trotter stopped him all right. You don't remember him telling you anything else about Brent?"

"What else is there?" Her mother's voice was wary.

Jeannie's eyebrows rose in advance of her mother's reaction, "Brent was angry because he found out he was adopted."

"Adopted?" Mrs. Fedorchak fell back against the sofa. "Are you sure?"

Jeannie nodded.

"I understand why he'd be upset," her mother said, pausing, "but even if he did just find out, what does that have to do with you?"

"Nothing except that Brent thought I already knew and that it was the reason I kept rejecting him. So in his fit of rage, he decided to try and steal the kiss I would never have given him."

Mrs. Fedorchak held an intense gaze on Jeannie. "It's time for a talk with Mr. Phillips and Brent."

Jeannie breathed out a sigh. "As awful as it was, I do kind of feel sorry for them. I can't imagine how traumatic it must have been for Brent to find out he wasn't a real Phillips after all. His life is never going to be the same."

"I have a feeling that's a good thing, though I still can't believe Brent's parents thought they could hide that kind of truth from him. Secrets like that don't stay quiet forever. Everyone knows a skeleton…"

"…kept in the closet will rattle its bones sooner or later," Jeannie joined in with her mother. "I told that to Mr. Trotter."

Mrs. Fedorchak returned a thoughtful smile before standing up, "I think we could both use a cup of tea right now."

Jeannie watched in amusement as she left to go into the kitchen. To her mother, tea was life's elixir, the antidote for any type of ailment. It wasn't until after their first sip that Jeannie spoke again. "Mr. Trotter has the letters from Grandma and Maria."

Jeannie's mother responded with a perplexed look. "Why?"

"He told the class today about how his great uncle ended up living in Perry. When he said he was able to read Russian, I thought he might be familiar enough with other languages to know which one the letters were written in. He agreed to take a look so I hurried home after school to get them."

"Did he know?" Her mother's question was filled with anticipation.

"He said they were written using the same alphabet as the Russian language, and that it might take some time, but he should be able to translate most of the words," Jeannie answered.

"Incredible," her mother said, initially seeming at a loss for words, but then she became more pensive. "That explains what you were doing at the school, but why was Brent there?"

"Brent blamed Mr. Trotter and the genealogy assignment for ruining his life and planned on confronting him about it." Jeannie then shrugged. "I think I just happened to be in the wrong place at the wrong time."

Moments of quiet passed while they finished their tea, giving her mother time to process what she had been told. "It's been a long afternoon. Why don't you go upstairs and rest while I fix something for dinner."

Jeannie didn't argue, and went up to her bedroom feeling as if her ankles were suddenly shackled with heavy chains. She fell onto her bed without caring that a pillow wasn't underneath her head. Within a few breaths, she was in a stage of sleep not even the doorbell could penetrate.

"Jeannie."

Jeannie blinked a couple of times as her mother touched her shoulder.

"Should I tell Jason you'll talk to him later?"

It only took hearing Jason's name for Jeannie to force her eyes open. "He's here?"

"He's waiting in the living room."

Jeannie sat up and ran her hand through her hair. "Tell him I'll be there in a minute."

Her mother smiled. "You look fine, but are you sure you're up to seeing him?"

Jeannie's nod prompted her mom to go ahead and leave the room. By the time she changed shirts and reached the bottom of the stairs, Jason had his back to her, looking at their old family portrait. As soon as he turned to look at her, Jeannie knew he had heard what happened. His expression was almost identical to what her mother's had been, a competing blend of anger and concern.

Jason spoke first, "Your mom said she needed to check something on the stove."

Jeannie's eyes shifted to the front door then back to him. "Do you want to sit out on the porch?"

Jason's head motioned his reply.

As soon as they were settled on the bench, she watched Jason brush his hand over his mouth and stand back up. He took a few steps before turning back around. "Sorry, I haven't been able to sit still."

Jeannie started to respond, but Jason was quick to continue.

"I've had to put up with the Phillips family for as long as I can remember, always having to be careful not to say or do anything that might ruin our chances of buying the property. But as of today, the rules have changed. Heaven help me if Brent were to show up right now."

That Jason's hands kept opening and closing didn't go unnoticed. Jeannie got up and walked over to him, then took both of his hands in hers and looked into his face.

"Jason, I'm okay."

"But it's not okay that he touched you."

Jeannie's response was calm. "Not in any way that matters. He's never cared about me, only his pride."

Jason seemed to relax enough to give Jeannie half a smile before his eyes met hers. "That goes to show how stupid he really is."

As if by a power much greater than their own, their lips drew together in a simple kiss, making Jeannie's heart feel like it skipped a beat inside her chest. She couldn't imagine something so tender and beautiful ever happening with anyone else. Their hands released as his arms wrapped around her waist in a hold Jeannie wished could last forever.

"I have a feeling your dinner is about ready, and I wouldn't want to keep you mom waiting," he said after a few moments.

Jeannie looked up at him. "I'll see you tomorrow then."

Jason kissed her on the forehead before he completely released his arms. "It won't come soon enough."

Jeannie went back into the house and into the kitchen, still feeling the warmth of his arms.

"Wasn't it freezing outside?" her mother asked as she set the plates on the table.

"A little," Jeannie answered. At least the weather was a perfect excuse for the rosy color she was sure her cheeks were wearing.

Her mother paused, seeming somewhat hesitant before she spoke again. "I was thinking about inviting Mr. Trotter over for dinner Friday evening. It's the least I can do to thank him for all he's done."

Jeannie's thoughts sped back to the last time her mother fixed dinner for someone new to Perry. "That's fine with me. What are you going to fix?"

"I haven't decided yet. Any ideas?" she lifted her shoulders with the question.

Jeannie opened the drawer to get the silverware and hide the smile that was spreading across her face. She turned back toward her mother, knowing the perfect dish to suggest.

"How about fixing chicken and dumplings?"

Chapter Thirty-three

Though it had only been a few days since the confrontation in the parking lot, by the time Friday arrived, it felt like an eternity had passed. It was Brent's first day back at school, and Jeannie noticed right away how different he looked. She was so used to seeing him puffed up by his overinflated ego, that without it, everything about him seemed small and insignificant. It was as if Brent Phillips no longer existed, and to an extent, he didn't.

Jeannie was thankful it was the weekend, but from the time she arrived home from school, she couldn't stop pacing the floor. She was already nervous that Mr. Trotter had accepted her mother's invitation and was coming for dinner. Then she read the note her mother had left saying she was leaving work early to go by the Phillips' home. Jeannie wished she were with her. As strong a woman as her mother was, Jeannie was afraid Mr. Phillips might try to bully her again. He had already kept her from getting the promotion she deserved.

Jeannie peered out the window another time hoping she'd see her mother's car pulling into the driveway. A glimpse of shiny red metal sent Jeannie running into the kitchen ready to shower her mother with questions as soon as she placed a foot through the door.

At the turn of the knob, Jeannie was already spewing, "How did it go?"

Her mother sat her purse on the table and removed her coat before answering. "It went much better than I expected. Brent acknowledged what he did was wrong, but I made sure he understood he wasn't off the hook that easily and that he owed his biggest apology to you. Then I confronted Mr. Phillips about the file I had seen."

"Which file was that?" With all that had happened Jeannie had forgotten.

"The one I came across when I was preparing for the promotion. All it contained was a handwritten note that I almost didn't read. Once I did, I realized it was the purchase terms for the property the Butlers have been leasing, written and signed by Mr. Phillip's father. It used to be a handshake was all it took to make a binding contract with an honest businessman. Thankfully, he did more than that and documented the agreement on a piece of paper I was lucky enough to find."

Jeannie took the next few moments to let the information sink in. "Well, if all this mess somehow ends up helping the Butlers finally buy their property, maybe it was worth it."

Her mother's response was more skeptical. "I wouldn't get your hopes up too quickly. Mr. Phillips was able to get the land appraised for twice the value that was agreed upon and has tried to deny the note his father wrote exists, even though he knows Mr. Lathrop saw it, too."

"It's hard to believe a father and a son could turn out so different from each other," Jeannie said with a frown.

Mrs. Fedorchak made a frown of her own, "Or two sisters."

The question hung in the air before Jeannie responded, "You're right, they're not that different from Maria and Grandma."

Her mother nodded then continued, "I think I passed Emma's car on the highway. It looked like she was headed to the Phillips house as well."

Jeannie gave her mother a knowing look. "It probably was. Ever since she found out Brent was adopted she's wanted to talk to him. I'm sure he could use a friend who would understand better than most people what he was going through. Emma's always been so crazy about him, and I never could figure out why. Maybe deep down she sensed they had this common connection."

Jeannie's mother sighed. "Life is full of mystery,"

"Well, it's no mystery that Thanksgiving is less than two weeks away and the genealogy project is almost due. I had hoped to have more information for it by now."

"There's a chance Mr. Trotter may still find something in the letters. Speaking of…," her mother's eyes shot over to the clock, "I better get started on the chicken and dumplings."

"While you're fixing dinner I think I'll take Nugget for a short walk. He looks like he needs one." Jeannie laughed as Nugget immediately went to the door in expectation. She was convinced dogs understood the English language better than most humans.

Jeannie grabbed her jacket and Nugget's leash from the coat rack and stepped outside. The truth was she needed the walk, hoping it would help her be less anxious about Mr. Trotter coming over. She knew it wasn't a real date, but if the evening went well enough, maybe it would lead to one. Emma would be so proud of her matchmaking thoughts.

After walking only a couple of blocks, Jeannie heard a deep sounding engine approaching from behind. She led Nugget away from the curb and onto the grass to make sure they were out of the way. A quick check over her shoulder revealed this wasn't just any vehicle closing in on her, it was Brent's.

As the truck slowed to a stop, Jeannie resisted the urge to turn and look. Even as she noticed the window lowering on the passenger's side, she pretended that she didn't.

"Hey, Nugget."

Jeannie's head whipped around at the unexpected sound of a familiar voice calling her dog's name. Emma greeted her with a smile, leaving Jeannie at a loss for words. She wasn't surprised to see Emma with Brent, it was that she hadn't been this close to Brent since the incident and she suddenly felt awkward.

"We were out for a drive and happened to see you two walking." Emma glanced at Brent then opened the door and got out. She knelt down and started petting Nugget.

Jeannie heard the engine shut off and the other door open and close. When she looked up, Brent was walking around the front of the truck to where they were.

Brent's eyes took a moment to find hers, but as soon as they did Jeannie noticed a difference. The flame of challenge that used to flicker in them was no longer there. "I want to say I'm sorry for the way I treated you the other day. I was angry and confused, but that's no excuse." He paused then added, "I hope you will accept my apology."

"Sure," Jeannie managed to say.

Emma stood back up and looked at her. "Call me later, okay?"

"I will after dinner." Jeannie watched them get back in the truck and drive away before checking the time on her watch.

Mr. Trotter would be at her house in less than thirty minutes. Giving Nugget the lead, the race was on, though Jeannie quickly realized she didn't stand a chance of winning. Four legs instead of two was a definite advantage.

She hurried to remove Nugget's leash and entered the kitchen trying to catch her breath. "Sorry, I took so long, Mom. I saw Brent and Emma on my walk."

The knife her mother was using to cut up the chicken stopped while she fixed her gaze on Jeannie. "I'm assuming he apologized?"

Jeannie let out an extended breath. "Yes and now I'm ready to forget everything that happened."

Her mother studied her as if checking to make sure she meant it. "Then we will. Now, if you'll set the table, I have just enough time to freshen up a bit."

The doorbell rang as her mother was coming back down the stairs, "I'll get it, Jeannie."

The next words Jeannie heard were, "Hi James, come on in."

Jeannie's hand paused as she set down the last fork. It sounded strange to hear him being called by his first name, though she supposed it would have been stranger had her mother called him Mr. Trotter.

"It smells wonderful in here, Laura."

"Thank you. Let me take your coat so you can make yourself comfortable on the couch or if you'd rather, you can come into the kitchen while I finish up the dumplings. Dinner shouldn't take too much longer."

"Since you offered, I think I'll join you in the kitchen. Maybe I can learn a thing or two about cooking."

Jeannie stood in the background watching the scene play out between Mr. Trotter and her mother, their smiles, their gestures. They seemed so unaware of her presence that by the time they turned around, their faces looked surprised to see her looking back at them.

"Hi, Mr. Trotter," she said.

"Hello, Miss Fedorchak," he returned the greeting, bowing his head slightly.

Jeannie grinned. "Do you think you could call me Jeannie for tonight?"

"I think I can do that," he answered with a grin of his own. "And how are you this evening…Jeannie?"

"Good," she answered. It sounded funny at first, but she liked hearing him say her name.

Jeannie followed them into the kitchen and leaned against the counter with Mr. Trotter while her mother spooned generous dollops of dough onto the bubbling broth.

"Do you like to cook, James?" her mother asked, placing a lid on the pot.

"I'm afraid I've never quite gotten the hang of it," he chuckled. "Fortunately for me, I met the Butlers soon after I arrived in Perry. Mrs. Butler has made sure I haven't starved ever since. I do believe one could survive off her chocolate cake alone."

Jeannie laughed in agreement. She knew all too well about that cake.

Mrs. Fedorchak flashed a smile at both of them. "That's the second time I've heard about this cake. I'm beginning to feel left out that I've never had any."

She turned her attention back to the pot and lifted the lid, sending swirls of aroma toward the ceiling. "The dumplings are almost done. Why don't you two take your seats in the dining room while I serve this up?"

Mr. Trotter walked to the chair at the end of the table. "Where should I sit?"

"Right there is fine," Jeannie answered. "We rarely eat at this table unless it's a holiday or a Monday."

Mr. Trotter looked both amused and confused. "Is there something special about Mondays in Perry?"

"No, I'm pretty sure we're the only ones in town that celebrate them." Jeannie giggled at Mr. Trotter's perplexed expression.

"Sounds like I missed something," her mother said, entering the room with bowls of steaming chicken and dumplings.

Mr. Trotter waited till she set the bowls in front of them then smiled. "Jeannie was just telling me about celebrating Mondays."

"Have you never celebrated one before?" Mrs. Fedorchak winked at her daughter causing them both to laugh.

"Now, it's my turn to feel left out," he joined in.

"Forgive us, James. It's just something we came up with a few years ago." Her mother went back into the kitchen and returned with the last bowl. "Let's eat while it's hot."

For the next few minutes, the only sounds were that of spoons scraping along the sides of the bowls.

Mr. Trotter looked over at Jeannie's mother, "That was some of the most delicious food I've ever had."

Jeannie watched her mother's cheeks turn a shade darker than her blush.

"Thank you," she answered. "Please, let me get you some more. There's plenty left for seconds."

"If you insist," Mr. Trotter said, pausing to smile, "Then maybe one of you will explain how you came up with celebrating Mondays."

Jeannie waited until her mother returned with Mr. Trotter's bowl and he began eating. "It didn't seem very fair that Monday was the day everyone seemed to dread the most. So we decided to make it a day to look forward to instead," she told him.

"It probably sounds silly," her mother added with a laugh.

Mr. Trotter shook his head while finishing his smaller second serving. "On the contrary, I believe every day deserves to be celebrated. There aren't enough of them as it is." His tone was almost wistful before he cleared his throat and continued. "I brought Maria's and Sophia's letters with me tonight in case this was a good time to tell you about them."

"Yes! Can you tell us right now?" Jeannie didn't even try to dampen her enthusiasm.

Mr. Trotter's answer was laced with caution. "I wasn't able to translate every word, but enough to learn a few important things."

"Why don't you two go ahead into the living room? It will only take me a minute to clear the table," Jeannie's mother suggested.

Mr. Trotter retrieved the bundle of letters from his coat pocket then sat in a chair across from Jeannie. "Some of these letters were written when your grandmother was about your age."

Jeannie could hardly keep herself still with the growing suspense. For some reason Maria had chosen not to burn these letters like she had everything else. Tonight, she hoped to finally know why.

Chapter Thirty-four

"I'm not sure where to begin," Mr. Trotter said after Jeannie's mother joined them.

"How about starting with the letters Sophia wrote first," Mrs. Fedorchak suggested.

Mr. Trotter nodded and opened the envelope on top of the stack. "This first one was sent to Maria at an address in New Jersey. In it, Sophia talked mostly about their twelve year old brother, Igor, who had been very ill."

Jeannie and her mother glanced at each other.

"My father had an uncle named Igor?" Jeannie's eyes widened with her question.

"Yes, but your father would never have known him," Mr. Trotter answered, pausing a moment. "Sophia wrote many words lamenting the lack of food and warmth that was needed to make their brother stronger, and then of the day he fell asleep in her arms and never woke up. She said the tears that had yet to dry from their mother's death would now have to be used to grieve for him."

While Jeannie tried to grasp the sadness her grandmother must have felt, Mr. Trotter continued. "It's in the next letter where Sophia revealed her excitement about coming to America and living with Maria in New Jersey.

Their father had remarried so she went to Germany to work in a factory. She said that by the time she turned eighteen, she would have enough money to buy passage."

Jeannie shook her head. "That seems so young to be traveling across the ocean by yourself, not knowing what lay ahead."

Mr. Trotter smiled. "Your grandmother was young, but she possessed great fortitude. She was as determined to make a better life for herself as Maria had before her."

Jeannie knew Sophia had been poor. What she hadn't understood was how poor. Her grandmother grew up unsure if there would be any food to eat or if there was enough wood to burn to keep them warm. As if those weren't enough of a hardship, she then lost her mother and her brother.

"Are you all right, Jeannie? You seem awfully quiet," her mother asked.

It took a moment for the question to intercept Jeannie's thoughts. "Sorry. I guess there's just a lot to think about."

"We can go over the rest of the letters another time if you'd prefer," Mr. Trotter said.

Jeannie had waited a long time for this moment. However much he had to tell them, she wanted to hear all of it. "No, I'm okay. There's just still so much that doesn't make sense."

She sat up straighter as if that might help to clear her confusion. "We had heard the story that Grandma's money was stolen the last night on the ship and that she had to return to Germany. But why would she have to go back if Maria was already in America and would be meeting her?"

The question hadn't hung in the air very long before Jeannie looked at Mr. Trotter. There was only one possible answer. "Maria never showed up, did she?"

Mr. Trotter met her gaze and shook his head. "And without money or a sponsor, she couldn't stay. Sophia's next letter was forwarded from Maria's old address in New Jersey to California. She was very worried about why Maria hadn't come and wanted to make sure nothing had happened to her."

Jeannie felt the well of resentment toward Maria grow even deeper. "Did Maria's letters explain why she left, why she abandoned her sister?"

"Only that she had made a terrible mistake, one she would have to live with for the rest of her life. Each of Maria's letters ended with 'Forgive me'," Mr. Trotter's voice softened with his answer.

"What could have been so important to Maria that she was willing to move clear across the country, especially when she knew her sister was coming?" Jeannie asked less forcefully this time.

"Whatever the reason was, it apparently didn't turn out well," her mother answered this time.

Several moments of silence followed before Mr. Trotter stood up. "I feel I should probably go now. I wish I had been the bearer of better news on an evening of such great food and company."

Mrs. Fedorchak stood and smiled. "Thank you, James, for everything. We appreciate all you were able to tell us tonight. Maybe someday we'll learn the rest of the story."

Jeannie rose and managed a smile of her own. "Thanks, Mr. Trotter. See you at school on Monday."

Jeannie's mother looked at her as soon as Mr. Trotter left. "You look exhausted. Why don't you go on to bed? There's only a small bit of cleaning up left to do in the kitchen."

Jeannie considered looking through the letters again that had been left on the coffee table, but the dizzying effects from Mr. Trotter's information had begun to take their toll. "I think I'll take you up on that."

Calling Emma would have to wait until the next day. She climbed the stairs looking forward to getting her pajamas on and slipping underneath the covers of her bed. But as soon as Jeannie's head sunk into the cushion of her soft pillow, she was reminded of having always known these simple comforts. They were something Maria and Sophia didn't have growing up.

Her mind began to beg the question whether hardship alone could make one person bitter and another grateful. Grandma Sophia found such joy in life, perhaps because she understood its fleeting nature, while Maria turned out so differently. There had to be another reason why.

Jeannie rolled onto her other side hoping that was enough to shift her thoughts to a more pleasant subject. It seemed to work as the memory of being in Jason's arms made her smile. Reliving the moment, Jeannie was soon caught in a realm between consciousness and weightlessness. She was only slightly aware of something ringing in the background.

Maybe another memory was trying to get her attention, or maybe it was simply the telephone. Before Jeannie could determine which one, however, the sound stopped, and she drifted on into a full, deep sleep.

Chapter Thirty-five

When Jeannie began to stir the next morning, it took a moment for her to remember that it was Saturday. Her eyelids felt heavy as she forced them open to look at the time. It was only 8:00 so she let them close again. There was nothing on her schedule she had to get out of bed for.

But memories from the previous evening soon started trickling back into Jeannie's mind until it was as if the floodgates had been lifted, demanding her thoughts to wake up. New questions rose to the surface like fish needing to come up for air. It was no use. Sleep was never going to return.

Jeannie put on a robe to go downstairs and found her mother in the kitchen already dressed and reading something off the notepad they kept on the refrigerator. "Are you going somewhere?"

Her mother's head shot up. "I didn't expect to see you awake this early."

Jeannie pulled a container from the refrigerator and poured some juice into a glass. "I started thinking about last night and couldn't sleep any longer. I figured I might as well get up and work on my genealogy project, especially since Jason's coming over tonight."

She finished her drink before continuing, "You didn't answer my question."

Her mother pulled off the top sheet then folded it and placed it inside her purse. "I think you better sit down."

Jeannie eye's narrowed on her mother's face for clues. Not finding any, she went and sat at the kitchen table. She was more curious than she was nervous. Her mother would be more upset if it was something awful.

"After you went to bed last night I got an unexpected phone call. You'll never guess from whom." Her mother's lips formed a firm line.

While Jeannie remembered hearing the ringing, it was still early for a Saturday morning. She tried to shake herself alert. "Was it Mr. Trotter? Did he forget to tell us something in the letters?"

"No, it wasn't James," her mother answered, seeming to purposefully avert her eyes.

Jeannie noted a smile in them, however, that her mother couldn't hide. "Then who was it?"

Her mother took in a deep breath. "It was your Aunt Maria."

"Aunt Maria?" The name never failed to make Jeannie shiver, more so now that it was getting closer to winter, but also because only the coldest person would abandon a sister when she was to arrive in America. It was because of her that her grandmother had to return to Germany, without money and all alone. "What did she want?"

A few breaths passed between them before her mother answered. "She's coming for a visit."

Jeannie was quiet while she processed the words she had just heard.

"Today," her mother added.

The last word threw Jeannie's mouth open in a state of disbelief. "How is it even possible for her to come today? And why would she?"

"I don't know why, Jeannie, except that we're all the family she has left. There was such desperation in her voice when she asked that I couldn't say no."

"She could have given us a little more warning besides the fact that family never seemed to matter to her before," Jeannie snapped. She closed her eyes a moment to collect her emotions. "Will she at least be gone in time for Thanksgiving so we can go to Uncle John's like we always do?"

This time her mother was quiet.

Jeannie didn't need to hear the answer to know this was going to be one of the worst Thanksgivings of her life. "What time do we have to pick her up from the airport?"

"Not until 2:00, but I plan on leaving here by 1:00. You don't have to go, though I would feel better if you were along."

"I'll be upstairs working then until it's time to go." Jeannie went back up to her room still bewildered. What made Maria think she and her mother had nothing better to do than put up with her porcupine disposition, and why now? It had been over two months since Grandma Sophia died.

Jeannie decided to get dressed, and then laid out everything she had gathered so far for her genealogy project. There was a copy of their last family portrait, then pictures of her mother's parents, and information of their ancestry back in Scotland.

The only item she had for her father's side was a copy of a map of Austria-Hungary to show where Grandma Sophia was from. Jeannie would have to use words to substitute for the pictures that were absent. While she still didn't know as much as she'd like to about her grandmother's life, the letters had revealed enough for her to tell a story about her courage and perseverance.

Jeannie was busy writing when she heard the front door close and hurried steps coming up the stairs.

"Jeannie," her mother was almost out of breath when she appeared in her room.

Jeannie set her pencil down and sat up. "Is everything okay?"

Her mother was still breathing hard. "I didn't realize how cold it had turned when I went to get the car warmed up."

"That will be a nice change to get inside a warm car. I guess I better get my shoes on if we're leaving."

"You don't understand, Jeannie. The car won't start."

Jeannie thought a moment. "Can't we jump start it?"

"That might work to get us to the airport, but I'd be too afraid once we turned the car off, it wouldn't start again." Her mother looked at her watch.

"Jason could probably borrow his dad's pick-up, but it would be a little crowded and it would take him awhile to get here," Jeannie considered as a solution.

"We don't have very long if we're to have any chance of making it in time for her arrival. I wonder if James would mind driving us." Mrs. Fedorchak looked at Jeannie as if seeking her approval.

Jeannie grinned. "You won't know unless you ask."

Her mother left to make the call while Jeannie finished getting ready. She could hear her mother's explanation of the situation to Mr. Trotter and grinned even bigger.

"He said he'd be right over so we better head downstairs to wait," she said when she returned to Jeannie's room.

Jeannie had hardly gotten her coat on when his car pulled up in front of their house.

"You don't know how much I appreciate this, James," her mother said after opening the door to get in and situating herself in the front seat.

"I'm glad you asked me. I know this can't be easy for either of you," he said, glancing in his rearview mirror to look at Jeannie, and then her mother.

"I hope you'll at least let me pay you for the gas it will take to get there and back," Jeannie's mother tried to insist.

Mr. Trotter smiled. "I'd rather just have more chicken and dumplings."

"Well, if it's food you prefer, I have a great recipe for lasagna."

"You won't have to twist my arm. Lasagna it is."

The needed laughter that followed the exchange was accompanied by more for the rest of the drive. Considering the reason they were going to the airport, they arrived in pleasant moods.

"I feel badly we're a little late. I told her we would meet her in the baggage claim area." Jeannie's mother picked up her step as the three of them hurried from the car.

"It's not your fault your car wouldn't start, Laura. I'm sure Maria's found a place to sit down and wait."

Jeannie's eyes scanned all the seating in the area after they entered the building. Further ahead she saw people pulling suitcases off the big conveyor belt as they came around. Nowhere was there anyone that looked like Maria.

By then all of their heads were turning in every direction searching for a woman Jeannie and her mother had described to Mr. Trotter as being short with curly grey hair. He had chuckled at the time saying the description fit almost every woman in her eighties he had ever met.

"She's got to be here somewhere if she was on that flight," Jeannie said, continuing to look.

"Sir," Her mother stopped a man in uniform as he walked by, "Have you seen an older woman who appeared to be waiting on someone?"

"There was one here a while ago," he answered then shook his head, "but I doubt she's the one you're looking for. This one was carrying on in a way no one here could understand. I don't know what language she was speaking, but it sure wasn't English."

The three of them exchanged wide-eyed glances.

"Where is she now?" Mr. Trotter stepped up.

The man pointed across the room. "There's an office over there where they first took her. She might still be in there."

"Thank you," Jeannie's mother said. He walked off before she posed the question, "Do you think it could be Maria?"

"It's not unusual for someone to revert to their native tongue when they're nervous or upset. There's only one way to find out for sure," Mr. Trotter answered.

Jeannie's mother led them to the door, pausing a moment at its threshold to listen. A voice inside the office could be heard asking loud and slow, "Ma'am, would you like some water?"

What followed was a succession of distraught mutterings.

The man had been right, it definitely wasn't English.

Chapter Thirty-six

Mrs. Fedorchak knocked.

When the door swung open, the man whose voice they must have heard speaking stood in front of them. "Can I help you?" he asked, clipping the question with impatience.

"We were late picking up a relative and were told she might have been brought here," her mother said.

The man stepped aside and motioned with his arm, "This woman?"

A head of gray hair was bent down still muttering what sounded like gibberish, though now it was interspersed with loud sobs. There was no doubt the woman in distress was Maria.

Jeannie's mother walked over and touched her on the shoulder. "Maria, please forgive us for being late."

Maria looked up and clasped her mother's arm. Her voice rose with renewed emotion, though her words were still not in English. Only one word was intelligible and that was Sophia.

Mr. Trotter knelt down in front of Maria and began speaking a few words in what sounded like the same language. The change in her demeanor was immediate. They communicated a short time longer, and then Maria turned to look at each of them. Her eyes were clouded with tears, but her expression was less panicked.

"Maria was afraid you wouldn't come." Mr. Trotter stood back up before adding, "She says she's the one who needs forgiveness."

Jeannie was relieved to hear Mr. Trotter speak in English again, but his translations did little to generate any feelings of sympathy toward her aunt. Now Maria knew what it felt like to be abandoned like Grandma Sophia had been.

Jeannie's mother turned to the man who had been waiting off to the side. "Thank you for watching her. We'll take her home now."

"No problem, Ma'am," he said in a manner revealing his eagerness to have his office to himself again. "Don't forget her luggage by the desk."

Jeannie saw she was closest to the suitcase and picked it up. It wasn't large or heavy which made her think Maria wasn't intending to stay long, at least not much past Thanksgiving.

Mr. Trotter helped Maria stand and led her out followed by Jeannie and her mother.

"Will you be all right while I go get the car?" Mr. Trotter looked at Jeannie's mother for an answer.

She nodded and smiled her assurance.

Jeannie wasn't as sure. With everything she had learned from the letters, it was hard for her to look at Maria without feeling angry. She didn't know how she was going to survive the hour drive back home with her much less having her stay in their home for who knew how long.

To make matters worse, Jeannie only had a few more days to finish her genealogy project. She wished she could just take Aunt Maria to class for show and tell instead. Maria could tell them first-hand how she was so caught up in her new life in America that she forgot to pick up her sister when she sailed over to join her a couple of years later.

Mr. Trotter pulled up outside and opened the car doors for them. Thankfully, Jeannie's mother offered Maria the front seat. She appeared more than willing to sit beside the man she didn't know, but who had come to her rescue.

Jeannie knew the ride home from the airport wasn't going to be nearly as pleasant as the one there. Everything about the cold and cloudy afternoon seemed gloomier with Maria in their presence. The air was thick with tension, discouraging anyone from speaking.

Surprisingly, it was Maria who broke the silence once they were on the highway. "How is it you speak Russian?"

Mr. Trotter's chuckle helped to lighten the mood, if only temporarily. "I'm afraid you've heard the best of what I know. What little I do speak I learned from my mother. She grew up in Odessa."

Maria's head bobbed with understanding. "Thank you for speaking what you knew."

"You're welcome." Mr. Trotter answered.

Jeannie had no desire to engage in conversation. What could she say to Maria, especially if it was forgiveness she wanted? *I forgive you for stealing my grandmother away from me...I forgive you for turning my past into a pile of ashes...and oh, I forgive you for now ruining a perfectly good Thanksgiving.* It was easier to close her eyes instead.

Not much more was said until they were back in town and Mr. Trotter pulled into their driveway. By then, the sky was spitting frozen pellets of sleet that were beginning to collect on the windshield.

"It looks like we made it home just in time. You all hurry inside, and I'll get the luggage," Mr. Trotter offered.

Jeannie's mother started helping Maria out of the car while Jeannie ran to the porch to unlock the front door. The drop in temperature gripped her fingers as she fumbled through her keys to find the right one. She opened it just as everyone was ready to step into a warm house.

"Where would you like me to put Maria's suitcase?" Mr. Trotter asked.

"You can set it in here for now. You've done so much already, James. I want you to get home before the weather gets any worse."

"I probably should at that. It was very nice to meet you, Maria. See you in class, Jeannie." Mr. Trotter stepped out the door followed by Jeannie's mother.

Jeannie didn't expect to be left standing in the room alone with Maria. It was difficult to look at her, but she was a guest in their home now and Jeannie would never want to appear rude. "Here, let me take your coat."

After Jeannie helped her remove it, she noticed how thin Maria had become and was immediately driven to ask, "Can I get you something to eat?"

Maria shook her head as tears threatened to fill her eyes again. "No, I've already caused you enough trouble."

Jeannie didn't know how to react. Her resentment of Maria ran deep yet here she was next to a woman who looked so much older and frailer since the last time she saw her. To still be angry seemed heartless.

The door opened then closed again quickly as Jeannie's mother re-entered the house. "Brr...I'm afraid winter's going to be arriving early this year." She looked back and forth between Jeannie and Maria. "Is everything okay?"

Maria simply nodded.

"Let's get you settled into your room where you can rest before dinner if you'd like. The guest room is right down this hallway," her mother said, leading the way.

Jeannie watched them go ahead before picking up Maria's suitcase. She ran into her mother on her way back to retrieve it. "I'll take it to her, Mom."

When Jeannie walked into the room, Maria was looking at the pictures on the wall. She set the suitcase by the chair.

"Thank you, Jeannette."

Jeannie looked at her, startled.

"I hope you don't mind me calling you that. It's the only name I ever heard Sophia use."

It was difficult to hear it coming from Maria. Nothing about the way she said it sounded the same, but Jeannie couldn't refuse her. Not now. She tried to smile then left to join her mother back in the living room.

"Jeannie," she said, pausing a moment. "I hope you don't mind, but I thought it would be nice to invite James for Thanksgiving dinner since he doesn't have any family here."

"Of course not, I like Mr. Trotter." With the nudge of a dare Jeannie added, "And I think you do, too,"

Her mother's eyes shied away then returned. "Is that all right? I mean...that I enjoy his company."

In what felt like a complete reversal of roles, Jeannie walked over and placed her hands on her mother's shoulders. "Mom, I know you think that love, like lightening, doesn't strike in the same place twice. But I happen to know you're wrong. Lightening does strike in the same place and there's a tree on our property to prove it."

Jeannie's mother dismissed the comments with a shake of her head. "I feel like a silly school girl. He's probably just being nice like a good friend would be." She took a breath before continuing, "Then I also feel guilty."

Jeannie was thoughtful before she responded. "I don't remember much about my father, but I know he would never think you were betraying him, nor would he want you to spend the rest of your life alone. And you don't need to worry about how I feel. I've been hoping love would strike you again for some time now."

Her mother look relieved. "Thank you. I needed to hear that."

"I'm going to go call Jason and let him know what's happened today. I don't think he should get out in this weather to come over tonight anyway." Jeannie started up the stairs then stopped and grinned.

"And by the way, Mom, I'm one hundred percent positive Mr. Trotter does not think of you as just a friend."

Chapter Thirty-seven

Patches of sleet on the ground the next day made Jeannie feel trapped in her own house. Normally she would welcome the opportunity to stay inside, warmed by a fire and a cup of hot chocolate. But not today, not with the still strained silence of Maria's presence.

Jeannie stared out the window by the front door, silently begging the sun to come out and at least melt what was in the streets so she could drive out to see Jason, or maybe even Emma. Jeannie had hardly spent any time with her since she always seemed to be with Brent now, but that was okay. With all that had changed, she found herself believing they were right for each other after all.

"There you are," said her mother walking up beside her, "I was beginning to think you had gone into hiding."

Jeannie turned to her mother and breathed out a heavy sigh.

"I know this is difficult." Her mother's words corresponded with the understanding on her face. "I am concerned about Maria, though. She doesn't look as though she's been feeding herself very well, if at all."

Jeannie nodded, "I noticed how frail she seemed, too."

"I have some vegetable soup simmering on the stove. If you'll get some spoons out, I'll let Maria know it's time for lunch. I'm hoping she'll eat more today."

Jeannie placed the last spoon on the table as her mother brought Maria in to sit down.

"I think there's nothing better than a bowl of hot soup on a day like today," her mother said as if she could tame the awkwardness with conversation.

Maria said nothing, but picked up her spoon to start eating. She was soon the first one to be finished.

"I'm glad you liked the soup, Maria. Let me get you some more." Jeannie's mother stood up to take her empty bowl to be refilled.

Maria started shaking her head. "No..." her voice caught, "I should never have come. I don't deserve any of this. I don't deserve you."

Jeannie and her mother shared a quick glance.

"What do you mean, Maria?" Jeannie's mother asked.

By then Maria was sobbing, and Jeannie feared another episode like the one at the airport. If she broke out in Russian again, they wouldn't be able to understand a word she said.

"Sophia never got angry with me, never told me what a horrible sister I was for not meeting her. But I couldn't...I was such a fool, and she still forgave me," New tears overwhelmed Maria's ability to continue.

Jeannie sat in her chair stunned by Maria's admission. Maybe now Maria would tell them her reason for not showing up.

"Why don't we go to the sofa where it's more comfortable, Maria," Jeannie's mother suggested.

Maria seemed to resist at first then accepted help up from the chair. The doorbell rang just as they sat down.

"I wonder who that is," her mother said, looking toward the front door.

"There's only one way to find out," Jeannie went to answer it.

The shadow through the curtains could almost have been Jason's, but it wasn't. When Jeannie opened the door, Mr. Trotter stood smiling at her.

"I hope I'm not interrupting anything. I happened to find this in the front seat of the car after I got home yesterday." He held out a scarf Maria must have left.

Jeannie's mother joined them at the door. "Please come in, James. You must be freezing."

Mr. Trotter accepted her offer and came inside the house.

"She's in the living room if you would like to give it to her," Jeannie said.

For having been so wrought with emotion only minutes ago, Maria's face lit up as soon as she saw Mr. Trotter.

"It's good to see you again, Maria. I didn't want you to think you had lost your scarf at the airport," he said, handing it to her.

"Thank you." Maria took the scarf and held it to her chest. "This was one Sophia gave me."

The mention of Sophia renewed Jeannie's hope that Maria would finish telling them what happened. She wanted to come right out and ask her, but not with Mr. Trotter there now.

"Why don't you stay and join us?" Jeannie's mother asked. "We were just enjoying the warm fireplace."

Jeannie watched Mr. Trotter sit down next to Maria on the sofa. She could tell Maria liked him, that something about him made her feel safe.

The fire crackled as Maria looked first at Mr. Trotter, and then her and her mother. "I have felt shame for most of my life. It is time I tell you why."

Jeannie didn't dare move as a stronger sounding Maria spoke.

"I couldn't wait to have Sophia in America with me and had sent her money to make sure she would have enough. And then a man named Henry Winston ruined everything." Maria's last words were almost spat with bitterness.

Memories flashed back in Jeannie's mind to when she had encountered the name Winston before. She had seen it on the magazine in Maria's home and again on the letters.

Maria's new strength was being challenged as tears began refilling her eyes. "He dreamed of us making it big in the movies and convinced me to marry him."

"Maria, you don't have to tell us..." Jeannie's mother started.

"No, you must let me finish. Please." Maria dabbed her nose with a handkerchief Mr. Trotter handed her. "I knew California was the new place for making movies, but I thought there was still time before we had to go and was planning to take Sophia with us. Then Henry showed me the train tickets. We were scheduled to leave the same day Sophia was to arrive."

The anguish Maria still felt was obvious.

"He promised me a friend would meet her and take care of her until she could join us. I should never have gone with him, but I found out I was expecting our first child. I didn't tell him until we were in California. Instead of being happy, he said he had no use for fatherhood or me. Two months later, I lost the baby."

Jeannie's mother held Maria by the shoulders. "I'm so sorry, Maria. What did you do then?"

"I worked very hard on my English and on my writing so I could have a job and still act in small roles. Then rumors started going around about some people in Hollywood being communists. I didn't want anyone to think I might be a communist, too, so I burned all the records, and hid everything else. Some days I was afraid to leave the house. The happiest moment in my life was when Sophia came to live with me, and I wasn't alone anymore."

Fear. That was why Maria kept the drapes in her living room closed, even if it meant living in darkness. But something else still didn't make sense to Jeannie. "Why were you so upset when we found Sophia's wedding picture?"

Maria was looking exhausted as she answered. "Did you not see I wasn't in the picture? I couldn't even attend my own sister's wedding. It was another reminder of all my failures."

Jeannie could hardly wrap her thoughts around how sad a life Maria had lived. It was clear now what her grandmother had meant when she said Maria needed her. She was the only one who knew how much guilt and loss her sister had suffered. What little love Maria had experienced came from Sophia.

Another look at Maria and Jeannie was determined that was going to change. "Aunt Maria, I don't think you brought a big enough suitcase for as long as you're going to be staying. We have Thanksgiving this week and then Christmas soon after that. Then of course there's New Year's."

Mrs. Fedorchak couldn't have given her daughter a bigger smile when Jeannie glanced at her.

"But I brought almost everything I have." Maria seemed worried.

"That's even better. We've been planning to take a shopping trip, haven't we, Jeannie?" her mother said.

Maria started shaking her head. "Oh no, I couldn't let you."

Mr. Trotter who had only been listening up to then suddenly began laughing. "Maria, I don't believe you stand a chance refusing these two. You might as well prepare yourself. It looks like you're going shopping for some new clothes."

Chapter Thirty-eight

With the weight of resentment gone, Jeannie felt like a new person over the next few days. She was also excited because it was Thanksgiving. There was so much she loved about the holiday, from watching the parade on television to eating until she thought she might bust. But it was waking up to the smell of pumpkin pie that she loved the most. Its spices of cinnamon and cloves never failed to enter her room and lure her out of bed in the morning.

Even though they were staying home this year instead of going to her uncle's, Jeannie expected to wake up to the same sweet scents. Instead, the air that penetrated her senses was filled with savory smells of sage and onions. Her nose led her down the stairs and into the kitchen where she found her mother basting a turkey and Maria kneading dough.

"You two are awfully busy this morning." Jeannie said, unable to stifle the yawn that followed.

"It's been a long time since I've gotten an entire Thanksgiving meal together on my own. I have so much to get ready." Her mother closed the oven door then swept her hair away from her face.

Jeannie frowned at her mother's flustered appearance. "How much food are you planning to make? There's only going to be four of us."

Her mother laughed as she bustled next between the refrigerator and the pantry. "The number never matters. You still need to have gravy, dressing, mashed potatoes, sweet potatoes, cranberry sauce, green beans, and corn, no matter how many are eating." Then smiling at Maria she added, "And of course, homemade rolls."

Maria's hands stilled a moment as she turned to look at Jeannie and her mother. "These were Sophia's favorite. I made them for her for as long as I could."

Jeannie heard Maria's voice falter and went to stand at the counter beside her, "I can't wait to try one."

"I hope they are still good. My hands aren't as strong as they used to be."

Jeannie was reminded of another time Maria needed help, finishing the pillow for her grandmother's casket. Making rolls for Thanksgiving dinner was at least a happier occasion. "If you show me what to do I'd be glad to help," Jeannie offered.

Maria began instructing Jeannie on how to roll the dough to the right thickness. Then proceeded to tell her how to cut out, butter and fold each circle before placing it in the pan to rise. By the time they had finished shaping all the dough, an hour had passed and the parade was half over. Jeannie would have offered more help, but in their small kitchen she figured the best thing she could do was give her mother and Maria more room to work.

She went into the living room and turned on the television to watch the remaining balloons and floats move across the screen. It felt strange at first not to be going to her uncle's house, but Jeannie wasn't as disappointed as she thought she would be. She found herself looking forward to their small gathering with Mr. Trotter and what may be days of leftovers.

"You might want to think about getting dressed soon," her mother said, walking in and seeing Jeannie curled up in the blanket her other grandmother had quilted for them.

Jeannie glanced at the clock. It was already past 11:00. "What time is Mr. Trotter coming?"

Her mother's manner was vague. "I told him to come around noon and that we would eat just as soon as I could get all the food on the table."

Jeannie left to go upstairs where she decided on a pair of gray pants and pink sweater to wear. It didn't take her much longer to apply her make-up and curl the ends of her hair. When she went back downstairs she noticed not much had changed. Other than a tablecloth, the table still wasn't set. There were no dishes, glasses, silverware…nothing.

She entered the empty kitchen where it looked like her mother had gotten more than just a little carried away by the Thanksgiving spirit. Pots and pans were everywhere yet she sensed something was still missing. Jeannie took in a deep breath while her eyes scanned the oven and the countertops. That was it. There was no smell of pumpkin pie.

"Mom," Jeannie called, almost running into her mother as she hurried out of the kitchen.

"What's wrong?" her mother reacted with immediate worry.

Jeannie shook her head in a quick response. "I didn't see a pumpkin pie. You didn't forget to bake one did you?"

Her mother started to speak, but it took a moment for the words to come out. "I thought it might be a nice change to have chocolate cake for dessert this year."

Jeannie was dumbfounded. It didn't occur to her that she hadn't seen a chocolate cake either. "What? No offense, Mom, but whoever heard of eating chocolate cake on Thanksgiving? You may have just insulted the pilgrims."

"What if it's Mona Butler's chocolate cake? I bet the pilgrims would have liked it," her mother challenged her.

"It's definitely the best I've ever eaten, but why would you have her make one for us on Thanksgiving of all days?"Jeannie's confusion had reached its peak.

"Well, when I invited the Butlers to dinner, Mona asked what she could bring. Since I'm the only one who hasn't tasted this special cake, I suggested…"

"Wait, you mean the Butlers are coming for Thanksgiving, too?"

The smile Jeannie's mother had succeeded in masking broke free. "I wanted it to be a surprise. That's why I've been waiting to set the table so you wouldn't wonder why there were eight places instead of four. We should probably hurry and finish don't you think."

Jeannie went to work getting the table ready and smiled as Maria came out of her room talking to Nugget who was following close behind as they went back into the kitchen. She was glad to see Nugget enjoying the extra attention as much as Maria seemed to enjoy giving it. Jeannie had just put the last glass down when the doorbell rang.

"Hi, Mr. Trotter," she said, letting him into the house, along with the colorful bouquet of roses he was carrying.

"I believe I could have found your house blind-folded as wonderful as it smells from your front porch."

By then Mrs. Fedorchak had joined them. "Maybe not as wonderful as those beautiful flowers smell. Thank you, James. I have the perfect vase to put them in. As soon as the Butlers arrive it will be time to carve the turkey."

"Speaking of the Butlers, it looks like they're already here," Jeannie said.

Her mother opened the door for them with Mrs. Butler and the cake leading the way. "Mona, you're tempting me to skip the turkey and go straight for the dessert."

Everyone laughed then Jeannie turned and gave Jason a teasing grin. "I suppose you've known about this?"

"Maybe," he grinned back.

"The food's about ready so why doesn't everyone go ahead and sit down at the table," her mother said.

Platters and casserole dishes streamed in from the kitchen until Maria brought in the last item, a tray of rolls fresh out of the oven.

"Maria, those look heavenly. I bet they taste as delicious," Mona said as Maria set them down in a space next to her.

Jeannie first saw the color appear on Aunt Maria's cheeks, and then saw her smile in a way she never had before. It was at that moment Maria's chiseled features seemed to melt, exposing the undeniable resemblance to her Grandma Sophia. For the first time, they looked like sisters. For the first time, Aunt Maria looked like family.

"I'd like to propose a toast to our hostesses with a simple Irish blessing," Mr. Butler said as he lifted his glass. "May joy and peace surround you, contentment latch your door, and happiness be with you now, and bless you ever more."

Each glass was then carefully clinked against the others.

"If I may I'd like to make a special one to my great uncle, Leopold Radgowsky, whose good fortune in ending up in Perry was passed down to me," Mr. Trotter added as he glanced to each of them around the table followed by another clinking of glasses.

"May I give a toast?"

All eyes turned to Maria whose eyes were sparkling with moisture.

"Of course, Maria, please do," Mrs. Fedorchak answered.

Maria lifted her glass. "To family."

"To family," everyone repeated.

One last clink gave way to the passing of food and conversation until no one could eat another bite.

Jeannie turned to Jason. "I could use some fresh air. Do you want to go outside on the porch?"

Jason followed her out to the swing and sat down beside her.

Jeannie looked at him and immediately spoke up. "The bank's Christmas party is next weekend, and I wanted to know if you would be my date."

Jason held his gaze on hers and let out a small sigh. "I can't."

That wasn't the answer Jeannie was hoping for. All that slipped out of her mouth was, "Oh," as she lowered her head.

Jason gently lifted her chin with his hand. "Hey, you should know by now I'd be your date anytime, anywhere. It's just that I've already made another commitment that night. You'll understand soon, I promise."

Jeannie nodded though she was sure her disappointment was apparent. "It's okay. You won't be missing much."

"Oh, but you're quite wrong, Miss Fedorchak." Jason smiled without taking his eyes off of hers. "I'll be missing going with you."

Chapter Thirty-nine

Mrs. Fedorchak walked into Jeannie's bedroom the night of the party and spun around in front of her. "Are you sure this dress looks all right?"

Jeannie stopped brushing her hair for a moment to watch. "It's perfect, Mom. Remember, I helped you pick it out."

"I'm sorry. I guess I'm just worried about making a good impression. This is my first event since the promotion," she said.

Jeannie smiled. "You look great, I promise."

Her mother turned to leave not seeming quite as convinced. "I'm going on downstairs. We only have about ten more minutes before it's time to go."

By then all Jeannie had left to do was put on her shoes. She got her black heels out of the closet and sat down on the edge of her bed to put them on.

"Jeanette."

Jeannie jumped at the sound of the voice, almost dropping a shoe. She didn't expect anyone to be upstairs, nor was her heart yet used to hearing her given name from someone other than her grandmother. When she looked up, she saw Maria standing in her doorway and was immediately taken aback. There was a pink tint to her cheeks, her hair had been curled, and she was dressed in the dark green suit they had purchased on their shopping trip.

"You look nice, Aunt Maria."

"Thanks to your mother. It's been a long time since I've been to a party. " She hesitated then lifted her arm toward Jeannie. "I have something I want to give you."

Jeannie took the envelope Maria held out to her and opened it. On a simple card was attached a stem of pressed roses. She had seen them once before.

"Those are the last roses Sophia had in her room, the ones you had me cut and put into a vase. I wanted to save them, and now I think you should have them."

Jeannie stared at how well preserved the petals were from the flower in full bloom to the bud that had opened ever so slightly since the last time she saw it. She noticed the writing underneath it and forced her eyes downward. Jeannie read it silently at first and then again out loud, "But he that dares not grasp the thorn, Should never crave the rose, from *The Narrow Way* by Anne Bronte."

The words seemed to demand silence until Maria spoke again. "That was one of Sophia's favorite quotes and one of the reasons she loved the flower so much. Do you know the other reason?"

Jeannie slowly shook her head, having no idea.

"Rose was her middle name. She saw a lot of herself in you, which is why she called you her little rose," Maria answered then smiled.

Sophia Rose ...what a beautiful name Jeannie thought. It was a reminder that she didn't have a middle name, but she decided from then on she would think of it as, Rose, after her grandmother.

Jeannie looked down at the pressed roses again. "Thank you, Aunt Maria. I will treasure these always."

She gave Maria a hug, relieved that she didn't feel as fragile anymore. Jeannie hoped for nothing but love to fill the rest of her great aunt's life. "It's time for us to enjoy ourselves at a Christmas party."

It wasn't until they were in the car on the way to the bank when Jeannie thought to ask her mother, "So who's the entertainment going to be this year, Maurice the Magician, or the Henderson Family Fiddlers?"

Her mother pretended to take offense. "I'll have you know I discovered some new talent from right here in Perry."

"Sounds great, Mom." Jeannie rolled her eyes and laughed.

Jeannie's mother laughed with her. "I think you're going to be pleasantly surprised," she said as they pulled into a parking space.

Jeannie helped Maria out of the car while her mother hurried on inside. "I'm sorry your friend wasn't able to come with you tonight, especially with you dressed up in that pretty gold dress," Maria said.

"Thank you, Aunt Maria, but it's okay," Jeannie smiled. "I know he would be here if he could."

They entered the bank and headed toward the large meeting room where lights and garlands had been strung across the ceiling.

Maria stopped before they went in. "I've never seen anything decorated so beautifully."

"Just wait till we start decorating our house for Christmas," Jeannie turned to her to say. "I'm glad you'll be here to help us hang all the ornaments on the tree."

Maria's entire face seemed to light up in response.

As they continued on into the room Jeannie looked around for anyone she might know. She waved at her mother who winked at her in return. It was then Jeannie heard *Jingle Bells* start playing, only it wasn't the usual rendition and it sure wasn't a recording.

Jeannie guided Maria to the corner of the room the music was coming from, walking around the group of people gathered close. She couldn't have been more astonished to see Mr. Trotter playing the cello with Mrs. Latimer, the librarian, and Mr. Fitzgerald, their neighbor, joining him in a trio. But there was an empty chair beside Mr. Trotter along with another cello, as if someone was missing from what was supposed to have been a quartet.

"Don't go making fun of my debut performance, now."

Jeannie jumped at the voice that whispered in her ear from behind and turned to see Jason dressed up and grinning at her. She glanced at the group before looking again at Jason. "You mean this is why you couldn't…That empty chair is…"

"For me," he nodded. "Mr. Trotter had an extra cello and offered to give me some lessons. I'll be joining them for a couple of songs later on."

Jeannie stared at Jason while her mind grasped what he had just told her. Then she grinned back at him. "I can't wait to hear them."

Jason laughed. "Believe me when I say I'm a beginner."

Becoming Rose

By then Jeannie's mother had walked over to join them. "Pretty good surprise, huh?"

"You're good, Mom. First, Thanksgiving, and then this," Jeannie crossed her arms.

Her mother just smiled. "Why don't you take Maria to get some refreshments? We have lots of food over there that needs to be eaten."

Jeannie watched her mother continue to mingle with the other bank employees and guests, knowing she was going to be great in her new position. They filled their plates with food then sat down to enjoy the music until it was time for the group to take a break. Jason then excused himself to go talk to Mr. Trotter while she and Maria stood up to get more to drink. Mr. Fitzgerald approached them before they had the chance.

"Hello, Jeannie. Who do I have the pleasure of meeting here?"

Jeannie looked first to Maria. "Maria, this is Mr. Fitzgerald, our neighbor. Mr. Fitzgerald, this is my Great Aunt Maria."

"I'm very pleased to make your acquaintance, Maria," he said with a warm smile.

Jeannie saw how embarrassed Maria became and quickly interceded. "Mr. Fitzgerald lives in the house on the corner and grows the most beautiful roses."

"Do you like roses?" he asked, looking at Maria.

Maria seemed to relax a little. "Why yes, I do."

"Then you must come see my garden in the springtime so I can show you...."

Jeannie eased herself out of the conversation to join Jason, who was standing beside Mr. Trotter and her mother.

"If I didn't know better, I'd think someone was doing a little matchmaking." Her mother's eyebrows rose in question.

Jeannie shrugged her shoulders with supposed innocence.

Mr. Trotter laughed. "I can't imagine a better gift for Maria than a new friend."

Contentment filled Jeannie's heart as Jason took her hand in his. There wasn't a part of her that wasn't happy, even after spotting Mr. Phillips there. He had done the right thing in the end, recommending her mother for the promotion and honoring his father's agreement with the Butlers to purchase the property. She knew Brent was still wounded, but hoped in time he would be able to forgive.

Jeannie had only to glance around the room to see how life was full of second chances. And that like the rose, forgiveness bore a beauty far greater than its thorns. Especially when it was simply…given…

A Note from the Author

A Wild West Show and a Russian Revolution, two things so unlikely to be connected, come together in the real life story of Leopold Radgowsky. While *Becoming Rose* is a work of fiction, it was inspired by this man who was a royalist refugee from the 1917 Russian Revolution.

Referred to as, "The Professor," Leopold spent the last ten years of his life in Perry, Oklahoma. He not only became the town's first full-time high school band director, but he also organized a civic symphony orchestra, attracting musicians from nearby cities to join. One of those musicians was a violin player from Stillwater, Oklahoma, who many years later, was my daughter's first teacher. It was from her that I first learned about Leopold.

The life of this man was as intriguing as how he ended up finding a home in the middle of the United States. The son of aristocratic parents, Leopold was appointed to conduct the Imperial Band of Russia, playing for the Russian artillery during World War I and for Tsar Nicholas II and his family on many occasions. But in 1917, the Bolsheviks, later known as the Communist Party, overthrew the Tsar and launched Russia into a revolution. As a Russian with royal heritage, Leopold had no choice but to escape or face execution.

After finding his way to Paris, Leopold met up with other Russian expatriates and organized a band. While the band was playing in London, they were hired by Col. Joe

Miller of the Millers Brothers 101 Ranch as part of a new Cossack riding feature in their Wild West Show. They toured Europe in 1926 before signing a contract to come back with the show to Marland, Oklahoma, the headquarters of the 101 Ranch. Two years later, however, financial difficulties caught up with the Miller brothers and the band was not rehired. What was once a sprawling 110,000 acre ranch that employed thousands of people, was heading toward bankruptcy.

Stranded in a foreign country, barely able to speak the language and mindful of the continued threat on his life, Leopold was persuaded to go to nearby Perry. Starting his new life teaching private music students, Leopold Radgowsky soon had the town brimming with music. At one time, he was declared "Perry's Most Valuable Citizen", and in 1936, he became an American citizen. Unfortunately, he died less than two years later in 1938. Not to be forgotten, however, the Oklahoma Bandmasters Association elected him into their Hall of Fame in 1990.

Leopold Radgowsky's life was one of privilege, courage and mystery, but he will best be remembered for capturing the hearts and admiration of a small town and the gift of music he gave them.

Watch for *Lillian's Locket,*
the next Legacy Novel,
coming soon

Lillian's Locket

*William placed the locket inside the envelope then
sealed it closed
Whether he returned home on the wings of man or
angels
He wanted her to remember him, always*

RAF Harrington, England, 1944…

Acknowledgments

Many thanks to…

…Elnor Ragan, a violin player and teacher in Stillwater, Oklahoma, who once told me she used to drive to Perry to play in an orchestra led by a Russian conductor. I was immediately intrigued and curious about him, wanting to know who he was and how he ended up living in a small town in Oklahoma.

…Leopold Radgowsky, a highly trained musician from Russia, who I can't imagine ever dreamed he would be in a wild-west show. His courage and willingness to make Perry his new home was a gift to many.

…Angela Box and Hadley Davis, two special readers, who took the time to proof the finished draft, and to my faithful critique group, an extra big thank you.

…my family, friends, and neighbors, whose continued love and support mean the world to me.

…my three daughters, whose own special gifts of music have been such a source of joy and blessing.

…Brandy Walker, my cover artist, whose time and creative insights I appreciate and value.

…all my readers, you have my deepest gratitude.

About the Author

Marilyn Boone is the award winning author of *Heartstrings*, her first Legacy Novel that won the category for Best Juvenile Book at the 2016 Oklahoma Writers' Federation Inc. annual conference. She is a former elementary school teacher, having taught in grades first through fifth. When not writing, she loves spending time with her family, as well as on a number of other creative and musical activities.

Becoming Rose is the second Legacy Novel, a stand-alone series of young adult inspirational novels, containing a little history, a little mystery, and always a little romance. Watch for another Legacy Novel, *Lillian's Locket,* to be released next.

Other works by
Marilyn Boone

Legacy Novels
Heartstrings

Book Contributor
Chicken Soup for the Soul: Reboot Your Life

Collaborative Novel
A Weekend with Effie

Anthologies
Seasons Remembered
Seasons of Life

Visit her on her website
http://www.marilynboone.com

Made in the USA
Charleston, SC
02 December 2016